A Time

A Time to Live

Carl Richardson

T

Copyright © 2024 Carl Richardson

The moral right of the author has been asserted.

Apart from any fair dealing for the purposes of research or private study, or criticism or review, as permitted under the Copyright, Designs and Patents Act 1988, this publication may only be reproduced, stored or transmitted, in any form or by any means, with the prior permission in writing of the publishers, or in the case of reprographic reproduction in accordance with the terms of licences issued by the Copyright Licensing Agency. Enquiries concerning reproduction outside those terms should be sent to the publishers.

This is a work of fiction. Names, characters, businesses, places, events and incidents are either the products of the author's imagination or used in a fictitious manner. Any resemblance to actual persons, living or dead, or actual events is purely coincidental.

Troubador Publishing Ltd
Unit E2 Airfield Business Park,
Harrison Road, Market Harborough,
Leicestershire LE16 7UL
Tel: 0116 279 2299
Email: books@troubador.co.uk
Web: www.troubador.co.uk

ISBN 978-1-80514-524-0

British Library Cataloguing in Publication Data.
A catalogue record for this book is available from the British Library.

Printed and bound in Great Britain by 4edge Limited
Typeset in 11pt Minion Pro by Troubador Publishing Ltd, Leicester, UK

1

The car's horn blared as the driver swerved to avoid the woman who had walked, apparently aimlessly, into the stream of traffic entering Tavistock Square from Woburn Place. The lights were green for the traffic, and the woman should have waited at the pedestrian crossing. Couldn't she see the lights? The driver pounded his horn again as the woman reached the pavement alongside the gardens. He had a brief impression of her face, startled, white and drawn. What demented individuals still walked the streets? But within a few seconds, he had forgotten about her as he focused on the next set of traffic lights ahead. Would he get through before they changed?

Anne Norton remained standing on the pavement as she recovered from the shock of having nearly been knocked down by the car. She was disoriented. She usually walked up to the zebra crossing on Upper Woburn Place, but on this occasion she had used the crossing near the entrance to the National Children's Infirmary, not registering, in her distraction, that it was a pelican crossing. She stood for a minute, holding one of the railings alongside the gardens with her left hand. She needed space to think, and the gardens, green under the trees, seemed to offer that. After a few moments, she walked along to the nearest entrance and into the gardens, eventually finding a seat on a bench under the trees. She bowed her head and, for a minute, she buried her face in her hands. For her, in that sun-dappled green space, there was only darkness – the darkness of not being able to hope.

Half an hour earlier, she had been sitting in a consulting room in the National Children's Infirmary, just across the road from the gardens in Tavistock Square. Sometimes she visited the Infirmary with her husband, Kevin. On this day, she had come alone, travelling in to London from their home in Didcot. Their four-month-old daughter, Emma, had been in the Infirmary for the last three weeks. When Emma had been born at the local hospital in Didcot, she had apparently been healthy and normal, and as their first child, Anne and Kevin had brought her home a few days later with intense joy. Her tiny form became the centre of their lives, in the way that only new parents can understand. At first, everything seemed to be normal. There were the expected sleepless nights, as Emma announced her need for feeding or a nappy change by crying and, as expected, that was sometimes stressful, especially for Anne. But they took these things in their stride as part of the greater joy of their first child. In substance their lives continued as before, but in spirit, their lives were transformed. Above all, baby Emma's arrival meant that she had become the future, their future – and their future would now be inconceivable without her.

Two months after her birth, Emma seemed to become a little quieter and less demanding, and the stress of sleepless nights was lessened in consequence. At first, this seemed like a blessing, but as time went on, it began to become evident that something wasn't right. To Anne, watching her daughter with a mother's eyes, Emma's quietness was more than just passivity – she was becoming weaker and less and less responsive. When these symptoms persisted, Anne had taken Emma to see their GP. The GP, Dr Greene, confirmed that there was something wrong, but was not immediately able to identify the cause. He had therefore arranged for Emma to go into Didcot hospital for tests, as soon as that could be organised. This meant that Anne would need to go into the hospital as well, in order to be with Emma. This had necessitated quite an upheaval in their domestic routine. Anne was still on maternity leave from her job at a local grocery store. Kevin, her husband, was an electrician who worked for a local engineering company. With Anne and Emma's absence, their little family unit was broken up, and with that, something of its sense of security and purpose was lost to them. It was never to return.

In Didcot hospital, Anne and Emma were given a room by themselves, off one of the wards. A series of tests had been carried out over a period of several days. The initial set of tests had been inconclusive however, and the junior doctor on the ward had ordered a further set of tests to try and identify the problem. The results of these had led to the involvement of the consultant paediatrician. This had led to yet more tests. During the time that this was taking place, there had been a noticeable worsening of Emma's condition. She was undoubtedly becoming weaker so that, sometimes, she didn't seem to have the strength to finish her feed, and would lie limp and listless in Anne's arms. Anne became very distressed, and when Emma showed no signs of recovery from this, she was placed in an incubator with an intravenous feeding tube. As Emma's condition continued gradually to deteriorate even after she had been put on the feeding tube, it was clear that there was something seriously wrong. Thus, the nightmare had begun.

The consultant paediatrician had asked to speak to Anne a few days later, when the results of the tests he had ordered had come back. He said that, although the latest tests were still inconclusive, they seemed to indicate that the problem was some kind of muscular or neurodegenerative disease. There would need to be more sophisticated tests to confirm the exact nature of this. He was therefore recommending that Emma be transferred to the National Children's Infirmary in London. As well as being able to carry out much more sophisticated tests, they were also better equipped to treat a condition of this kind, he had explained.

Anne had no option but to agree to this. It was becoming clear that what was affecting Emma was a serious problem, not some minor ailment. Kevin had also reluctantly agreed, when he had come to visit them that evening. The consultant paediatrician had already contacted the National Children's Infirmary about Emma's case, so once Anne and Kevin agreed, he had immediately arranged for Emma to be transferred. Two days later, Emma had been moved by ambulance, accompanied by Anne, to the building on Tavistock Square in London which housed the National Children's Infirmary. The change of location had also brought about a change in Anne's relationship with her baby. Since Emma was now entirely dependent on an intravenous tube feed, it was deemed no longer necessary for Anne to be with her all the time. It was the beginning of the separation that she sensed was now imminent. When she had requested a room, or at least a bed, where she could stay, she had been told that, because of limited space, such facilities were restricted to parents who were directly involved in the care of their child, which Anne no longer was, since Emma was now on artificial support. The decision caused her a great deal of distress. She was, as a mother, at the stage of being in the most intense relationship with her baby, and suddenly to be separated from her like that was nothing less than cruel, she felt. Kevin had been angered by the distress this had caused her, and the following day he had gone with her to the Infirmary to demand that Anne should be allowed to be with Emma. The Infirmary Administrator was unmoved, however, and reiterated that shortage of space meant that there was no bed available. He also observed that, as Emma was now under the Infirmary's jurisdiction, the Infirmary would have complete discretion as to the circumstances of her care. It was an early indication of the trouble to come.

From being in a situation where she was with Emma all the time, Anne was now having to travel into central London every day and back to Didcot in the evening, in order to spend as much of the day as possible with Emma. But now, she was only a visitor – an outsider who was allowed to come and see her daughter only on sufferance by those who now had charge of her. Neither the doctors nor the nurses nor the administrative staff seemed to care about the effect that this would have on her.

A further week had thus elapsed, while yet more tests were carried out and the results awaited. Anne continued to travel into London every day, to spend as much of the day as she could near to Emma. Most evenings, Kevin would also travel in to see his daughter, and they travelled back together. On the Thursday evening of that week, just before Anne left to return home, the ward sister called her over to say that the consultant in charge of Emma's case wished to speak to her the following day and wanted to be sure that she would be there. The following day, Friday, Anne travelled in to the Infirmary as usual. Shortly before 11.00, she was called through to the consultant's office.

"The results of the latest series of tests have now been received," he had said, once she had sat down. He spoke in a matter-of-fact way, hardly looking at her, as though what he was saying was small talk of no importance. "What they have confirmed is that this is a case of Behrens-Hillingdon Syndrome. This is a very rare condition, fortunately with only a few cases reported each year. Behrens-Hillingdon Syndrome is an autosomal recessive disorder that causes a general and progressive neural degeneration. From case histories, where an individual is affected, it always manifests in infants soon after birth, and the full extent of progression in an affected individual is normally seen within a period of twelve to fourteen months from first symptoms. There's no known cure for the condition. One or two case studies cite treatments that may mitigate some of the symptoms in some cases for a limited period, but there are no reports of treatments that halt the progression of the condition. All of the reported cases of Behrens-Hillingdon Syndrome have been fatal within fourteen months, regardless of any mitigating treatment. I'm afraid this is the timescale that you will likely be facing. We can offer treatments that have been authorised by the NHS, but these will essentially be no more than palliative care."

At first, Anne could not take in what she had just heard. It seemed unreal – beyond belief. The doctor had been speaking in a matter-of-fact manner, as if what he had been talking about was something of little or no importance, which only added to her sense of disbelief. Eventually, she managed to say:

"Are you telling me … are you telling me that … Emma … is going to die?"

"I'm afraid I am, yes. It's a genetic condition for which there's no known cure, and such treatments as are available are not reported to prolong life-expectancy. At best they may mitigate some symptoms in a few cases. I can well understand that this news will be very distressing for you, but I'm sure you'd prefer me to give you the facts as I have them."

Still the same bland, matter-of-fact manner.

"Surely there must be something?" she said. "I can't believe that in this day and age, that there's nothing at all that can be done."

"There's no known cure for the condition, the progress of which is inevitable, so treatments that might mitigate some of the symptoms temporarily may not necessarily be appropriate. I can give you some literature about Behrens-Hillingdon Syndrome which will show you that there's general agreement among medical authorities about these conclusions. I realise that this will be difficult for you to come to terms with, but it would be entirely wrong of me to build up false hopes where there are none."

It was all so civilised, as if the death of a child was just something that any civilised person should take in their stride. After all, did he not do so every day?

She tried once more.

"Is there nothing you can tell me to give me any hope?"

"I'm afraid it would be improper of me to do so. As I've explained, none of the authorised treatments has any effect in altering the course of the condition. I would advise that it would be better in the long run if you were to reconcile yourself to the inevitable."

He gave her some documents, evidently about the condition whose name she had barely taken in. It was an indication that the appointment was over. Perhaps this was also difficult for him, but the bland, detached manner didn't seem to say so. She didn't look at the documents. She was in a state of confusion. When she had eventually left the building, she was still confused and distraught and, without thinking, she had walked out onto the pedestrian crossing. After the shock of the near-miss, the blaring car horn, she had retreated instinctively into the refuge offered by the gardens, seeking only to be alone. For a long while, she sat on the bench under the trees, her face buried in her hands. At first, there was only darkness. But before leaving the Infirmary, she had gone up to the intensive care unit to see Emma. She had been asleep in the incubator she was in, her little form almost still: only her tiny, uncertain breaths signalling that she yet lived.

Seeing her tiny form lying there, her Emma, her little girl, produced a surge of emotion in Anne such that she became momentarily disoriented. How could she even contemplate letting her die? It was unthinkable. If love had any meaning, it also meant the will, the unshakable will, to live, in oneself, in one's child, in and through those one loved, to the uttermost breath of life.

Now, as she sat on the bench, her mind exploded with light in the intensity of a single resolve.

"If it is humanly possible in this world, you will live, my darling – you will live!"

2

At first, there was no light.

In the days following the interview, Anne and Kevin had scoured the internet for everything they could find about Behrens-Hillingdon Syndrome. The initial impression was confusing, as most of the search results were on medical sites which discussed the condition in abstruse technical language which meant little to them. Articles intended for general readers were very few, and they appeared to confirm the view of the consultant who had spoken to Anne. They struggled further with the technical language on the medical sites, hoping to find an indication that there might be another narrative, but it was like trying to read a foreign language. Meanwhile, events began to take their course. With no positive treatment being given to her beyond palliative care, Emma's condition continued to deteriorate.

The following week, the consultant asked to speak to Anne and Kevin together. Kevin couldn't immediately get time off work, so it was a couple of days before they were able to see the consultant together. They were kept waiting for some time in the waiting room before they were called. Once they were seated, the consultant wasted no time in coming to the point.

"I assume you've had time to study the information I gave you," he said, looking at Anne.

"Yes, we have, but I'm afraid it wasn't very helpful," Anne replied after a moment.

"It contained all the relevant information about the condition," the consultant said, looking displeased. "It's all taken from documented cases of the syndrome. It's the best information I can give you about the condition."

"But it doesn't give any information about new or experimental treatments," Kevin answered.

"The advice we give, about any condition, always includes all the relevant information about it, including all treatments that are approved by the NHS. In the case of this condition, Behrens-Hillingdon Syndrome, there is no known cure, and there are no known treatments that alter the inevitable course of the condition. I realise this is hard for you to face, especially as it's your first child, but you must see that it's best to accept the reality of the situation, and face the decisions that have to be taken, however difficult they may be."

"We've found references online to possible new treatments that aren't mentioned in the information you gave Anne."

"I can assure you that the information I've given you includes all valid treatments for this condition. There may be research projects into the condition, which is probably what you're talking about, but a research project is not the same as a new treatment. We can only work within NHS guidelines, and with treatments that those guidelines have authorised. Unfortunately, as I said just now, none of the treatments for Behrens-Hillingdon have more than a palliative effect – they don't alter the course or the outcome of the condition. Since the outcome is inevitable, the sad reality is that you are going to have to come to terms with that. What I wanted to talk to you about today was to agree the best way of dealing with the inevitable. I understand that this will be hard for you to face, but the baby is severely unwell, and there is no point in needlessly prolonging her suffering."

"What are you saying? That we should just let her die?" asked Kevin. There was anger in his voice.

"I'm afraid it's not something that can be avoided. What I wanted to talk to you about today was to agree the best way of bringing about the inevitable, minimising the suffering of the child."

"What does that mean? That you want us to agree to let her just die, without making any attempt to save her? Well, I can tell you now that we don't consent to that."

"I'm afraid it's inevitable that she's going to die, and soon. That's what I've been trying to tell you," the consultant said blandly. "You both need to understand that what we have to agree on now is the most humane way to bring her life to an end, because I'm afraid that there's nothing that can be done to save her."

"Oh, yes, there is," said Anne, her voice low with emotion. "I've seen things on the internet." She got to her feet. "I'm not listening to any more of this."

Kevin also got to his feet.

"You're trying to tell us that there's no alternative but that she must die. Well, I know that there are alternatives, and I'm telling you that she's going to live."

The days that followed were a trauma of emotional turmoil. Emma was still in the National Children's Infirmary, but it was becoming increasingly clear that if she stayed there, she would die, because the consultants there had neither the desire nor the intention to save her. In order to save Emma, they had to find an alternative. This resulted in a further intensive search of the internet, following up every possible lead as far as they could. As before, this was made difficult by the arcanely technical nature of the subject matter. All the material on the internet about Behrens-Hillingdon Syndrome had been written by medical professionals for medical professionals, with no concessions to the ordinary reader. Much time had to be spent in trying to translate these texts into some form of understandable English in order to be able to assess whether or how they might be of help. Some of the articles were also in foreign languages, and they had to use machine translators on the internet to render them into some sort of English. Trying to decipher this material was doubly difficult, but it was one of these sources that eventually provided them with a lead.

As the search intensified, and they began to focus on those leads that seemed the most promising, they noticed two or three names which kept cropping up in the articles and the medical references attached to them. Finding out more about these individuals, and trying to assess how likely it was that they might be of any assistance if they were contacted, was almost as difficult as trying to understand the medical articles themselves. All of them had impressive-looking career histories and even more impressive-looking bibliographies, even if the details of these meant little to a lay person. But there were few glimpses of the individual personalities behind the academic careers and bibliographies.

Eventually, however, as their understanding of the subject matter developed, one name in particular began to stand out from the rest. He was a doctor and a professor. The details of his work were difficult to understand, but insofar as they could understand them, he was developing a new therapy for Behrens-Hillingdon Syndrome, which appeared to promise positive results. They talked over the best way of making contact with him and, after some discussion, decided that the best way was by email.

It took some time to draft the email as they debated the best approach, and it was redrafted and reworded several times before they agreed on the final version. Anne had wanted to include as much detail about what had happened as possible, but Kevin thought that too much detail, making the email very long, would be off-putting to the reader. Eventually, a final version was agreed. They read it through again.

"Is it OK? Have we got it right?" Kevin asked.

Anne nodded. She reached out and pressed the 'send' button.

3

Sandor Zentai read through the email again, his interest quickening as he did so. It was one of those moments when, looking back, one understood that something significant had happened – a turning point. Even at this moment, he sensed that this was going to be a decisive case. He reached for a notepad and began jotting down points that would need to be elaborated or checked before he replied to the email. His initial response to this would be important, especially if events in this case followed the pattern of recent, similar cases. This time, he thought, if it was humanly possible, events would be different.

Dr Sandor Zentai, a specialist in neurodegenerative diseases, was a senior professor at the Hungarian Institute of Medical Research in Budapest. As well as being a leading clinician in his field, he was also probably the world's foremost authority on Behrens-Hillingdon Syndrome. Behrens-Hillingdon was a difficult field of research because cases were rare. Cases which did occur were not always accessible to researchers such as Dr Zentai:

sometimes they were misdiagnosed as something else and, even when correctly diagnosed, all too often the hospital concerned would not allow experimental treatments to be used. Sandor Zentai had seen babies die because of this, needlessly in his view. Given the rarity of the condition, it was inevitable that experimental procedures would feature prominently in the possible treatment options for it, but because the babies almost invariably ended up in large hospitals run by the state or by large medical institutions which tended to be ill-disposed towards treatments and procedures outside their established norms, it was difficult to get experimental treatments for Behrens-Hillingdon even considered, let alone accepted. It seemed clear from the email that that was very much the situation in this case.

He began drafting a reply to the email, breaking off to check some of the details of the case. He paused to reflect for a few minutes, thinking about a conversation that had taken place some nine months earlier. From his first impressions of this case, it looked possible that this might be the opportunity that had been discussed in that conversation. Potentially, therefore, this case was extremely important. The email from the Nortons indicated that things were already well advanced, so time was likely to be short.

A week later, Sandor Zentai was walking through the main concourse of Terminal 5 at Heathrow, the destination of his flight from Budapest. Much had happened during the intervening week. His first reply to the Nortons had generated an emotional response as they realised that he was both sympathetic and willing to help in whatever way he could. They quickly developed a good relationship, even via email. It was as well that they did. The major development that week was that the Infirmary told the Nortons that they proposed to end Emma's life support and "allow her to die a natural death, in her best interests". The Nortons had immediately appealed against this to the relevant NHS Trust. Their appeal was immediately rejected. It was clear that the Trust, and the NHS, was fully behind the Infirmary's decision. The Infirmary, and the NHS Trust then applied to the High Court to approve the appointment of a guardian to displace the Nortons as the lawful parental authority for Emma. At that point, no date had been set for the initial hearing. The Nortons had engaged a solicitor, although they could ill afford to do so. These developments resulted in a fairly intensive exchange of emails, as Sandor did his best to advise and guide the Nortons on how best to respond. Events were following a course that he had seen too often before, and he knew that, without intervention, the outcome was likely to be only too predictable.

They met in the main lobby, near the information desk. The Nortons were both clearly nervous as he shook hands with them. This was an important moment for them. Sandor had booked into one of the main airport hotels near Heathrow, so after a brief conversation, the Nortons made their way back to their car and proceeded to the hotel, while Sandor completed the arrival formalities and then went over to the car hire company's office to collect his hire car. An hour later, they were able to meet in much more congenial surroundings in Sandor's hotel room. Despite all the emails they had exchanged, they still needed to get to know each other on a personal level. Fortunately, there were no problems – they got on well from the start.

The Nortons brought Sandor up to date with the latest developments, including letters from their solicitor about developments in the case. This included correspondence about ending Emma's life support and the attempt by the Infirmary to appoint their own guardian for Emma.

The immediate issue, however, was Sandor's forthcoming visit to the Infirmary as the Nortons' medical adviser, to carry out a formal medical examination of Emma and then to discuss her case with the Infirmary's consultants and staff. This was the main purpose of his trip to London. Sandor showed the Nortons letters and other documents he had received from the Infirmary, the NHS and the Department of Health, and they discussed the visit in detail. It was evident from the correspondence that Sandor's visit was regarded as an unwelcome intrusion into a process, the outcome of which was already regarded as a foregone conclusion as far as the Infirmary and the authorities were concerned. This impression was also evident to Anne and Kevin Norton when they read the correspondence.

In a general discussion about the situation, Sandor gave examples from previous cases he had been involved with to illustrate that this was a recognisable trait in most hospitals and the bureaucracies that supported them. There was a strong tendency within such institutions, to resent outside interference of any sort. This was reinforced by the knowledge these institutions had that their decisions would almost invariably be upheld by the courts in cases where their authority and judgement in relation to clinical care was disputed, something which, for Sandor, had been borne out by experience. Not only did this almost always lead to an attitude of arrogance, but it also strongly reinforced institutional prejudice against experimental new treatments which they had not been involved with. This was clearly what they were seeing now, with Emma's case.

This led to a discussion about the new experimental treatment for Behrens-Hillingdon Syndrome that Sandor had been developing. He explained the treatment in some detail, as far as possible in layman's terms: in particular, the technique he had been using to insert new sections of DNA into cells to replace damaged or missing DNA. The technique had originally been pioneered by two Russian scientists, Vladimir Karyagin and Mikhail Patolichev. They had only conducted live trials of the technique on animals. The only trials they had conducted in relation to humans had been on *in vitro* cell cultures. These had, however, indicated that the technique worked, at least in principle. Sandor had replicated these experiments himself, and then developed them further for the purpose of applying them to the treatment of Behrens-Hillingdon Syndrome. From this stage, in the ordinary course of events, a number of further stages had to be passed before live human trials could be considered. However, two factors influenced the situation in this case. The first was that cases of Behrens-Hillingdon Syndrome were very rare. The second was that there was no alternative treatment for the condition that had any effect.

Eventually, this had resulted in Sandor being contacted about his experimental work in relation to an actual case of Behrens-Hillingdon. The case had occurred in Nicaragua, in a baby born to a couple in a poor district of the provincial town of Chinandega, about seventy miles north-west of Managua. The facilities at the local hospital, where the baby had been taken, were very basic; however, by chance, the possibility occurred to the doctor on the ward that this might be a case of Behrens-Hillingdon Syndrome, even though he had not come across a case personally. A series of blood samples had been sent to the Ministry of Health in Managua, and the doctor's diagnosis was eventually confirmed. Since no effective treatment for Behrens-Hillingdon was known, that seemed to be the end of the matter.

However, the doctor, having had his diagnosis confirmed, investigated further, researching the available information about Behrens-Hillingdon. His attention was quickly drawn to Sandor Zentai as one of the leading authorities on the condition. After reading the published research literature, the doctor decided to contact Dr Zentai to see if he might be able to help in this case. Sandor was immediately interested. An exchange of several emails and two long phone calls followed. It became clear from these conversations that the condition was evidently far advanced in this case, which meant that the likelihood of Sandor's treatment having any effect was at best minimal. Nevertheless, since the doctor was willing to consider the experimental treatment, Sandor decided it was worth a try.

A few days later, Sandor and two members of his research team made the long flight out to Managua, where they arrived in the middle of a thunderstorm. From

Managua, a hire car took them the seventy miles or so to Chinandega. The following morning, at the hospital, Sandor carried out a detailed examination of the child. The examination quickly confirmed his impression from the phone calls and emails that the condition in this case was far advanced, and the outcome was inevitable. The baby was no longer conscious and was barely being kept alive by the life support system he was on. All that remained was to see if the treatment had any measurable effect on the condition of the baby at all. The decision to do so, however, was one made under the pressure of circumstances. Cases of Behrens-Hillingdon were few and far between, and he had made a long journey in order to see this one. At that moment, the idea of not giving the treatment a trial, even if it could not change the inevitable outcome, was one which he scarcely considered. In other circumstances, with more leisure to weigh up the pros and cons, he might have decided differently; but at that moment he had no doubts.

They set up their equipment in a room they were given just off the ward where the baby was, and once the necessary preparations were made, the experimental treatment began the following day. Sandor had been at pains to explain the situation to the baby's parents – that he could not now stop the inevitable outcome and could only try to see whether the treatment had any effect at all. Not speaking Spanish, he had to go through an interpreter and could only hope that they fully understood. He would need at least a week before he could be sure that test results would show whether the treatment was having any effect.

But fate dealt him bad luck at this point. Two days after the start of the treatment there was an outbreak of MRSA on the ward. Four children on the ward succumbed, including the baby being treated by Sandor Zentai. Once infected, the baby stood no chance, being already in a severely weakened state from Behrens-Hillingdon.

This led to a crisis with regard to the status of the treatment. Although it was clear that the baby had died of MRSA – as had the other children – and MRSA was recorded as the cause of death on the death certificate, it was also recorded elsewhere on the certificate that the baby was receiving an experimental treatment for Behrens-Hillingdon Syndrome at the time of death. When the death certificate was filed in the local public records office, some bureaucrat there noticed the reference to the experimental treatment and raised a query about it. The query was passed to the local coroner's office, which decided to pursue the matter and ordered an inquest to be held. Sandor and his team had returned to Hungary by this time and were initially unaware of these developments. Since the focus of the inquest was the experimental treatment used, it was inevitable that Sandor would be called as a witness. Sandor was instinctively cautious. The experimental treatment had not caused the baby's death, so an inquest focusing on it would almost certainly be a negative development. After taking advice, he responded by saying he would only agree to be a witness by video link from Hungary. He had someone he could trust and who spoke Spanish to act as interpreter.

The inquest was held in the coroner's office in Chinandega. Due to the time difference, it was late evening in Budapest. Those actually present included the coroner, his assistant and two clerks, the doctor on the ward who had the baby as his patient, a representative of the hospital administration, and the baby's parents and two other family members.

The coroner's assistant began the proceedings by reading out the brief for the inquest. This referred to the death certificate which had been issued for the baby by the hospital. The coroner then took over. He returned to the matter of the death certificate and clarified that the principal reason for the inquest having been called was the reference on the certificate to the experimental treatment the baby had been receiving at the time of his death. He turned to the ward doctor and asked if he could clarify whether the wording on the certificate meant that the experimental treatment may have been a contributory cause of death. This had led to an unexpected argument between the doctor and the representative of the hospital administration. When the doctor had signed the death certificate, a standardised document, the primary cause of death was given as MRSA, exacerbating a pre-existing medical condition: Behrens-Hillingdon Syndrome. However, in a section for additional information, it was mentioned that the baby had been receiving an experimental treatment for Behrens-Hillingdon. The ward doctor asserted that when he signed the certificate, he had not intended that the experimental treatment should be regarded as a possible cause of death. The hospital administrator countered that the reference to the treatment was added to the section on the certificate listing possible contributory causes of death because it might have been a contributory factor, given that it was an unlicensed treatment. An argument ensued, which was cut short by the coroner, who said that the issue of the treatment was the subject of the inquest.

When the proceedings moved on to examining the experimental treatment, Sandor was asked to explain the treatment in detail. He was requested to put his explanation in layman's terms and avoid the use of medical jargon. Sandor was told, on asking, that neither the coroner nor any of his staff present were medically qualified. Having explained the treatment in general terms, he was asked what negative consequences might be possible from the treatment. Sandor explained that, since the treatment was designed to correct a specific genetic fault, any consequence would relate to that, and he was not aware that there were any. The only possible negative consequences would be from deliberate overdose of the serum used in the treatment, and that had not happened. When asked what effect the treatment had had on the baby, Sandor explained that he would have needed at least a week before he could be sure of detecting any significant change in the baby's condition as a result of the treatment. The two days that he had had to administer the treatment was too short a time, and he had not detected any significant change. The most he could say was that one of the biometric measures he was using had shown a very slight movement in the right direction, but from this on its own, it was not possible to draw any definite conclusions one way or the other. When the coroner asked again if there could have been any negative effects from the treatment, Sandor answered that if there had been, the biometric measures he was using would have recorded that.

This led to an objection by the hospital administrator, who said that the biometric measures might not have been comprehensive enough. The possibility of undetected negative consequences could not be ruled out, he said, which was why he had added the reference to the experimental treatment as a possible contributory cause on the death certificate. Sandor asked if the hospital administrator was medically qualified. The man prevaricated, but the ward doctor intervened to say that the administrator was not medically qualified, but only a bureaucrat. This led to another heated argument, which was again cut short by the coroner. It seemed as if the coroner did not want attention to be drawn to that point.

On being questioned himself by the coroner, the hospital administrator made the point that he had opposed the use of Sandor's treatment on the child because it was unlicensed and still experimental, but he had been overruled by the ward doctor on the request of the child's parents. Because his office was responsible for processing death certificates, he had used this to ensure that the experimental treatment was not only mentioned on the certificate, but also in such a way as to indicate that the experimental treatment was at least a possible contributory cause of death. This led to a further protest from the ward doctor, which was again cut short by the coroner.

By this point it was becoming evident to Sandor that the coroner was steering the inquest in a particular direction. The ward doctor, in giving his evidence, confirmed his view that the primary cause of death had been MRSA infection, with the consequences of Behrens-Hillingdon Syndrome being a contributory factor, but that there was no evidence that the experimental treatment had been a contributory factor. Originally, the reference on the certificate to the experimental treatment had been under a separate heading of 'other information'; it had not been listed on the certificate as one of the causes of death, even as a possible contributory cause. His view of the treatment was that it offered a slight chance of hope in an otherwise hopeless situation. The treatment appeared essentially benign, and because the baby's parents were desperate, he was willing to try it if it could be arranged.

In his statement, Sandor reiterated the point that at least a week would have been needed for the treatment to have had any significant effect on the baby's metabolism. Two days would not have been enough for any significant effect, positive or negative.

Proceedings were then adjourned.

An hour later the hearing resumed, for the coroner to deliver his verdict. The coroner, in the summary of his verdict, said that while it was likely that MRSA and the effects of Behrens-Hillingdon Syndrome were the primary causes of death, it was his finding that the experimental treatment could not entirely be ruled out as a possible contributory cause. He therefore ruled that the hospital administrator's amendment to the death certificate be formally endorsed by the court to reflect this verdict. Sandor immediately registered a protest, saying that there was no medical evidence for such a ruling, or for any change to the death certificate. The ward doctor concurred, and also registered a protest about the death certificate being amended without his consent. The coroner was unmoved however, and ruled that his verdict would stand.

This incident proved to be a significant problem for Sandor in his attempts to gain acceptance for the experimental treatment, as he explained to Anne and Kevin Norton.

"As you will no doubt have seen from your research on the internet," Sandor said, "this case has been used on a number of occasions to prevent the use of my treatment. This is despite the fact that neither the coroner at the inquest, nor any of his staff at the time, were medically qualified. That's why I have explained this case to you in some detail."

"We have noticed that, yes," said Kevin. "But as we see it, as Emma's parents, anything such as a new treatment that might offer some hope should at least be looked at. We can't understand why anyone would want to block something like that from even being considered."

"The reasons are complex, but I think the main reason is a consequence of the power of established bureaucracies. Most hospitals are part of large, well-established bureaucracies, and in countries where parents have few, if any, rights over their children and the state has overriding powers, these hospitals, these bureaucracies, become arrogant about their ability to wield the power of life or death over those in their care. It's what I have seen many times before, and it looks as if that's what we're seeing again in Emma's case. Whilst we must go through the official procedures, we should do so in the knowledge that, as far as officialdom is concerned, the matter is already closed and the outcome is a foregone conclusion. I have faced this too often before without a plan for an alternative course of action. This time, we will have a plan."

4

Two days later they met again at Sandor's hotel, before proceeding into London to the National Children's Infirmary. Much would depend on what happened on this day. Sandor briefed them about what he expected to happen.

At the Infirmary, once they were on the ward, they were met by the ward sister. After introducing Sandor, Anne and Kevin were directed by the sister to go straight to the unit where Emma was, which they did. Meanwhile, the sister escorted Sandor along a corridor to an office, where he was told to wait. Presently, the sister returned, accompanied by the Infirmary's senior administrator and the consultant who was in charge of Emma. After briefly introducing them, the sister departed again, and they sat down, with Sandor facing the other two across the office desk as in a formal interview.

From the outset, the atmosphere was polite but frostily hostile. Sandor opened the conversation by saying that he had been engaged by the Nortons as a medical adviser with regard to Emma because of his research reputation relating to Behrens-Hillingdon Syndrome. They had done this because they had encountered problems with the Infirmary's response to the fact that Emma had Behrens-Hillingdon. He had been glad to accept the engagement, both to assist them in a very difficult situation, especially as this was their first child, and also because every case of Behrens-Hillingdon that was treated was important for increasing medical knowledge of the condition. The senior administrator asked Sandor what problems he was referring to.

"First of all, they are concerned about the fact that the Infirmary lacks expertise in relation to Behrens-Hillingdon," Sandor replied. "You don't appear to have anyone on your staff who has published research into the condition. Such things matter when the condition is so rare."

"All our staff are highly skilled in the treatment of sick children, which is why we are one of the leading institutions in the field in this country," the senior administrator replied.

"So you say. But the fact remains that none of your staff has published research into Behrens-Hillingdon. Secondly, despite this lack of specialism, there is increasing concern about the Infirmary's attitude towards the Nortons and their concern for their child. In particular, this relates to attempts to obstruct them from making decisions about the treatment of Emma. This has led to a situation where they no longer have confidence in the Infirmary for the treatment of their child."

"I'm afraid I don't recognise the narrative you're describing," the senior administrator responded. "At the

National Children's Infirmary, we pride ourselves on giving the highest standards of care and, in particular, we are always guided by what is in the best interests of the child."

"I'm not sure if I recognise the narrative you're describing," Sandor replied evenly. "The child's interests would clearly be best served by taking guidance from the leading authority on the particular condition, as defined by published research."

"Our experience and expertise as an institution means that we are very well-equipped to judge what is in the best interests of a sick child in our care, a fact that has been borne out on numerous occasions by the confidence in us shown by the highest medical and judicial authorities."

The tone of the exchange was bland and polite – they might have been discussing the weather. But the gloves were now off.

"You're evidently of the opinion that it's in the child's best interests for her life support system to be switched off, and for her to die," Sandor continued. "It seems as if you have already made up your minds about the outcome."

"Since there's no cure for the condition, such a conclusion is unavoidable. It's therefore in the child's best interests to end her suffering as soon as possible."

"There was no cure for many diseases before antibiotics were discovered. Time and again, research has provided new treatments for previously untreatable conditions. Where a new treatment has become available, it would be in the child's best interests to be given the chance to try it."

"I'm not aware that there are any such new treatments for this condition."

"That's hardly surprising given that none of your staff have any published research into Behrens-Hillingdon. I have been working on just such a treatment for several years and have reached the stage where clinical trials are appropriate. I've consulted extensively with the child's parents, and they are agreeable for a trial to go ahead."

"I assume you are referring to the treatment that resulted in the death of the child in Nicaragua," the senior administrator said with a look of contempt.

"That child died from MRSA, as did other children on the ward at the same time. He had not been receiving the treatment for long enough for it to have had any effect. The child's death certificate was altered, against the wishes of the ward doctor, to make it look as if the treatment may have contributed to the child's death. It was altered by bureaucrats who were not medically qualified."

"So you say." The look of contempt was still there. "All we have to go on is the official documentation, which shows your treatment as a contributory cause of death."

"The document is invalid with regard to that matter, since it was altered after being signed off by the ward doctor, by individuals who were not medically qualified."

"It must be so inconvenient when your reputation always goes before you."

"If that's the level you choose to operate on, then there isn't much point in attempting to have a conversation with you."

"As a reputable institution, it behoves us to protect our good reputation."

"Meaning?"

"Meaning that we cannot permit an unauthorised and unapproved procedure, especially one with a doubtful record, to be given to a patient in our care."

"The Nortons have requested that Emma be given the treatment I've developed in the hope that it might make a difference to the outcome. The main reason I'm here is to examine her with that in mind."

"You may examine her if you wish, but as I've just made clear, we will not permit an unauthorised treatment to be given to a patient in our care."

"The Nortons have made it clear that they want this treatment to be given to Emma. I think that there's a good chance that it can change the outcome. If you will not permit the treatment to be given to her here, then they will move Emma to an alternative medical facility that will permit the treatment to be given to her."

"That isn't the situation."

"I'm not sure what you mean by that. They've made it clear to me that they want Emma to receive this treatment. If that can't happen here, they'll move her to another medical facility."

"That isn't going to happen. She isn't moving from here. If necessary we'll get a court order to enforce that. Now that she's a patient in this institution, we will decide what's in her best interests."

"But … she's their child … their daughter …"

"Fortunately, Britain is a country where the state decides what is in the best interests of a child and has the power to enforce that. If we have to apply for a court order to prevent the child from being moved from here, and to confirm our decision to end life support, it's a foregone conclusion that the court will take our side in the matter. There's plenty of legal precedent for that."

"The Nortons are just trying to save their daughter's life."

"In Britain, the state has authority over children, which is absolutely necessary to protect children from irresponsible parents who might subject their children to unnecessary suffering."

"Even if an alternative treatment might offer a chance to save the child's life?"

"That's our decision to make, not theirs. In this case, our decision is that no such alternative treatment exists. Even without the damaging record of the Nicaragua case, the procedure you are offering is completely unproven as well as being unauthorised. It isn't an option as far as we're concerned and certainly doesn't alter our view that the best interests of the child are served by ending life support as soon as possible. You should be in no doubt that our decision is final in this case."

"I find your assumption of having a monopoly of clinical knowledge extraordinary," Sandor said slowly. "As is your assumption that you have a right to enforce it on anyone in your care."

"We are one of the leading institutions in the country, so it's natural that the judicial authorities and the state follow our guidance in these matters. And in Britain, it's the state that decides the fate of a child, and what's in the child's best interests, not uneducated parents."

In other circumstances, Sandor might have continued the argument. He certainly felt angry enough to do so. But it was clear that he was facing a brick wall – the confidence of hubris that comes with unlimited state power. On this occasion it was enough simply to record the hubris as part of what was happening.

A few minutes later, Sandor was being escorted by the ward sister down the corridor to the room where Emma Norton was. The room was a single-bed ward, equipped as an intensive care unit. Anne and Kevin Norton were already there and rose to greet Sandor when he arrived. In a side annex he donned mask, gown, cap and gloves in preparation for the examination. He fixed his mobile phone into a special clip attached to the cap so that he could record the process. When he was ready, he returned to the main room and went over to the bed where the little girl lay looking up at him.

"Hello, Emma. We're going to win this one – I promise you," he said to her gently.

He began by checking the readings on the various monitors attached to Emma, recording them on his phone. After checking that everything was in place and in order, he proceeded with the examination slowly and methodically, recording a running commentary on his phone. He spoke in Hungarian, partly for his own convenience, and partly because he knew it would irritate the ward sister, who was recording the examination on her phone, and her bosses, who would have to go to the trouble of getting a translation. As part of the examination, he took a small blood sample and a saliva sample which he transferred to his medical case, which lay open on an adjacent table. He also took a close look at the life support equipment, paying particular attention to the various connections. At the end, he took a careful look around the room. After returning briefly to the side annex, he rejoined Anne and Kevin, who had lingered for a few moments more with Emma, and they all left the room together.

Half an hour later, they were back in Sandor's hotel room.

"This has been a very informative visit, in a number of ways," Sandor said to them once they were settled. "Firstly, and most importantly, my initial impression from my examination of Emma is that the condition is not as far advanced as I had feared, and that leads me to be optimistic at this stage that she will respond to the treatment. I won't be able to confirm that until I've had the blood and saliva samples analysed, but my initial impression is favourable. If the analysis confirms what I think, then we have good reason to be optimistic about the outcome."

"But will they allow the treatment to be given to Emma?" asked Kevin.

"That's the difficult part. When I spoke with the senior administrator and the consultant at the Infirmary, they made it clear that they would not allow the treatment to be given to Emma at the Infirmary." He recounted the conversation.

"So, they haven't changed their attitude, then," said Kevin. "As you know, they've already started legal proceedings against us. If they haven't changed their attitude, and they still intend to stop Emma from receiving the treatment and stop us from moving her, what are we to do?"

"It's clear that they are not going to change their attitude," Sandor said. "Any plans we make must be based on that assumption. Because of what has happened in the past, I have given a great deal of thought to what must be planned to ensure, as far as humanly possible, that Emma receives the treatment and is given a chance to live. This case, Emma's case, has become of absolute importance to me. What we plan must address the different possible contingencies, but it must be based on the course of events that is most likely to happen."

"But doesn't that mean accepting that they are going to win?" Anne said. "They have the power because the authorities, the courts, will back them in what they want to do, which is to switch off Emma's life support."

Sandor shook his head.

"It's precisely because that's what they want to do, and because that's what they are confident that they will be able to do, that Emma's case is going to be different, especially if the sample tests confirm my expectation that the treatment will change the outcome for Emma. What the Infirmary is planning for Emma has happened too often in the past, and in other countries besides Britain. One reason why Emma's case is going to be different is that other individuals besides myself have become aware of her case and have taken an interest in it, and one individual in particular. I don't want to say too much about him at this stage, but I'm confident that there's going to be a good outcome for Emma, mainly because this individual has taken a keen interest in her case."

"Is this person a doctor?" Kevin asked.

"No. He's a businessman. I can't say too much about him because he doesn't want his identity to be revealed at this stage, although you will get to meet him in due course. He was made aware of Emma's case and was put in touch with me through a mutual acquaintance. His interest stems from his conservative Christian religious beliefs about the sanctity of life and his conservative political views about the excessive power of the modern state, particularly in relation to freedom of the individual and civil liberties. He was particularly incensed by similar cases in Britain in the last few years where the authorities colluded with the hospital to ensure the ending of the baby's life by withdrawal of life support, against the wishes of the parents and despite the offer of alternative treatment. When he heard about Emma, he was very determined that, if it was at all possible, the same thing should not happen again, and Emma should be given the chance to live. To a large extent, it's because of his support and determination that I'm optimistic about the outcome for Emma."

"How will he be able to help?" asked Anne.

"Well, as I said, he's a businessman. He's extremely wealthy – a billionaire several times over. In the first instance, that means that he'll fully cover your costs in any legal action taken against you by the Infirmary or by the authorities. You'll have the best legal representation money can buy."

"But if the courts are biased, we might lose the case even so."

"That's true, unfortunately. And under the current circumstances, it has to be seen as being more likely than not. But there are two reasons for fighting the case. The first is that we might win, even if that's against the odds. The second is that it gives us time. When I had a conversation with the businessman, he said he had given a lot of thought to the situation, given the outcome of previous similar cases. When he decided to take an interest in Emma's case, he said that, this time, things must be done differently. If we were to win the legal battle, he is prepared to fund Emma being transferred to my Institute in Budapest to receive treatment there. Realistically, however, we have to accept that the odds are against the authorities and the courts allowing that to happen. In anticipation of that, there has to be an alternative plan if things are to be different this time. There has to be a Plan B, which involves alternative medical facilities in a safe location beyond the reach of the British authorities and courts, and a means of getting Emma to that location safely. Although my businessman friend will fund any costs involved in fighting a legal case in the courts, his main focus has been on providing alternative medical facilities, and a means of getting Emma there safely. This time, there is a Plan B."

5

Back in his laboratory in Budapest, Sandor was able to confirm his initial impression from his examination of Emma. Tests on cells from the blood sample he had taken confirmed that Emma would respond well to the treatment. When the test results were complete, Sandor looked at them with satisfaction. This information now cleared the way for the main plan of action – which essentially had been Plan B from the beginning – to be put in motion.

On receiving the test results, Sandor sent out a number of messages. The first was to the Nortons, advising them of the test results. He then sent messages to those of his colleagues who were involved in the plan, advising them that action was now imminent. Finally, he sent a message to the man who was making the plan possible.

Sandor's message to the Nortons included detailed information about the next steps in this part of the plan as it involved them. As a result, the Nortons immediately filed a request to the Infirmary for Emma to receive Sandor's treatment. The Infirmary's inevitable refusal resulted in further legal action by the Nortons' solicitor to allow the treatment to be given. The Infirmary had already applied to the High Court to allow them to appoint a guardian to displace the Nortons as parental authority, in order to facilitate the Infirmary's decision to end life support. A date for a court hearing had not been set, but the action by the Nortons' solicitor now resulted in a date being set by the High Court for a hearing. As well as giving a focus to the legal process, this also provided a more specific timeframe for Plan B.

Sandor had emphasised to the Nortons that it was important that no mention should be made to their solicitor of any Plan B. Since the solicitor was not involved in Plan B, it was essential that all dealings with the solicitor should be confined only to the legal process surrounding the court case. With a date set for a hearing, this now began to take its course. On the Monday after the date for the hearing had been announced, the Nortons went to see their solicitor to be briefed on the case. Their solicitor was aware that they were receiving financial support from a private source to help fight the case, but the Nortons insisted that this was just a well-wisher who sympathised with their plight. There was no mention of any other involvement. It was a point of interest, however, as it meant that the solicitor was hoping to engage one of the best London barristers to present their case in court. This was one of the points to be discussed at this briefing.

The solicitor, Arnold Jenkinson, went through the main points of their case.

"At this stage, we're mainly responding to the actions taken by the National Children's Infirmary in restricting your right to arrange for Emma to receive the treatment you feel will give her the best chance of life," he said. "An alternative treatment is available, from a leading specialist in Emma's condition, but the National Children's Infirmary is preventing that treatment from being given. The details of the defence, and the way the case will be handled in court, will be decided by your barrister, but the case will undoubtedly focus on these two points: the alternative treatment and the primacy of your parental rights. Because the treatment is from a leading specialist, we will be placing the onus on the National Children's Infirmary to justify their actions. They may question Professor Zentai's credentials. We will be questioning theirs. We will also be challenging their attempt to usurp your parental rights. It's perfectly clear that you're very caring parents, and their attempt to usurp your role as parents is intended to serve their own interests, not those of Emma. This will undoubtedly be a challenging case, and much will depend on the barrister, but I'm confident that we can win.

"With regard to the barrister, I've been in communication with Roger Galbraith KC, one of the leading human rights barristers in London, who's expressed an interest in taking the case. He'll be expensive, but if you were able to afford it, then I think that if anyone can win this case, it will be him."

"Let us have the details, and we'll check and come back to you," said Kevin.

Afterwards, despite the upbeat views of their solicitor, Anne felt depressed: oppressed by a sense of powerlessness in the face of an all-powerful bureaucracy. Sometimes she felt overwhelmed by it. That evening, she and Kevin travelled to London to visit Emma. For Anne in particular, each visit was an intensely emotional experience, seeing again the baby she had brought into the world and nurtured, now trapped in this nightmare. On the ward, they found Emma asleep in her cot, the now-vital life-support systems attached to her. They sat together, holding hands, looking at their sleeping daughter. They were now all of them on trial as a family – little Emma was on trial for her life, and Anne and Kevin were on trial for their love for their daughter. Their inquisitor was an all-powerful leviathan, monstrous in its malevolence, and supreme in its hubris that it could do whatever it wanted to them. Having fixed them as prey, this leviathan would pursue them until it had destroyed them, in order to demonstrate to the world that it was all-powerful. Anne gripped Kevin's hand and closed her eyes in fierce thought.

"Why can't they just leave us alone...?"

Approval for engaging Roger Galbraith as barrister in the case was quickly confirmed once Sandor had relayed a message to the Nortons that whatever funding was needed would be available. A couple of days later, Arnold Jenkinson contacted the Nortons to advise that he had forwarded a brief to Roger Galbraith, who had agreed to take the case. From this point, the process was now in the hands of the court administrators, but at least a date for the hearing had been set. As was customary, Arnold Jenkinson acted as intermediary between the Nortons and Roger Galbraith. Jenkinson also advised that he was arranging a meeting at which the Nortons could be introduced to Galbraith at his London chambers.

For Anne, the most important event of the following week was an unexpected return visit to London by Sandor. Sandor was scheduled to make periodic visits to London to check on Emma's condition, but this visit was unexpected because it was arranged at short notice. The reason given for this visit was to allow a colleague of Sandor to examine Emma. Anne in particular was always pleased to see Sandor. His confidence that there was going to be a good outcome for Emma was infectious, and Anne's spirits were always lifted when he visited.

As usual, the Nortons met Sandor at Heathrow. Sandor introduced his colleague as Dr Peter Jones, a biochemist who specialised in human cell biology, who was currently working at UCLA. As they shook hands, it occurred to Anne that Dr Jones didn't look much like how she imagined an academic and scientist. He was powerfully built, like an athlete, and his keen blue eyes seemed much more purposeful than those of an academic. He reminded her of someone, and she puzzled for a while, trying to remember who it was.

They lunched together at the airport, and that afternoon they went into London to visit Emma at the National Children's Infirmary. Every visit was now fraught with emotion for Anne, and this visit was no exception. On reaching the ward, Sandor and Dr Jones donned gowns and masks. Sandor proceeded to carry out a methodical examination of Emma, including noting the readings on the various monitors attached to her. Dr Jones stood and watched but did not take an active part in the examination. Sandor noted that Emma's condition had deteriorated, meaning that it was essential that she started to receive treatment soon. Her muscle response had fallen by several points since his first examination of her.

Afterwards, they all met in Sandor's hotel room. The mood was sombre as Sandor described the deterioration in Emma's condition.

"If Emma doesn't start receiving treatment in the next three weeks, then I'm afraid that the deterioration in her condition may become irreversible," said Sandor. "Whatever else happens, it's essential that she starts receiving the treatment. Time is now a critical factor."

"We still have the court hearing to go through," Kevin said. "Is there going to be enough time?"

"I don't know. We have a good case and a first-class barrister and, in any fair hearing, I'm confident that we would win. But even if we win this hearing, the other side are likely to appeal. We have to be prepared for that."

6

Wednesday of the following week was the first day of the court hearing. The case was being held in the High Court in Westminster. The plaintiffs, the National Children's Infirmary Trust, were petitioning the court on two counts: firstly, to have Kevin and Anne Norton removed from all parental authority over their daughter, Emma, and replaced by a guardian appointed by the court and nominated by the Infirmary Trust; secondly, for the court to uphold and confirm the Infirmary's decision that it would be in Emma's best interests to have all life support withdrawn and for her life to be terminated as soon as possible.

Details about the petition and the hearing arrived at the Nortons' by post, with additional information about the hearing and the defence case from Arnold Jenkinson. For both Kevin and Anne, looking through all the paperwork, it seemed as if they were facing a vast machine which was bearing down on them, unstoppable in its vastness and supreme in the knowledge that the outcome was already a foregone conclusion and that there could be no hope, despite all the encouraging words from Arnold Jenkinson. It was only Sandor's infectious optimism which kept them going at this point, and his rock-steady confidence that Emma was going to receive the new treatment.

On the day before the court hearing, the Nortons travelled into London with Arnold Jenkinson for a meeting with Roger Galbraith at his chambers at Lincoln's Inn on Chancery Lane. Galbraith was part of a world that Anne and Kevin had little or no contact with. He was in his forties, dressed in a three-piece suit, worn slightly casually, which nevertheless added to a natural air of authority. Galbraith dominated the meeting, partly because he was in his own element and also because he had a naturally ebullient personality. Being in his element, however, meant that it was clear that he saw the case purely in terms of the legal arguments. This was a particularly interesting case, which he had taken up with enthusiasm, but the enthusiasm was primarily about the challenge of a difficult legal case in which his opponent, another member of Lincoln's Inn and a familiar adversary, would be representing the plaintiffs. It was part of a great game, whose purpose was essentially the game itself rather than any consequences in the real world. For all his presence and eloquence, he was, for Anne and Kevin, a figure from another world.

The following day, they again travelled into London with Arnold Jenkinson for the start of the hearing. Much of the morning was taken up with administrative procedures and form-filling, giving them authorisation to enter the building. Shortly before lunch, there was a brief meeting with Roger Galbraith, who was now wearing court dress, with wig and gown. He commented that they had been less fortunate than they might have been in the choice of judge, but he was still confident that they had a strong case.

After lunch at a nearby restaurant, they returned to the Royal Courts of Justice. The initial session of the hearing, being a short afternoon session, was confined to procedural matters, followed by opening statements by counsel for the plaintiffs, followed by counsel for the defendants. Counsel for the plaintiffs, Clifford Scholes KC, outlined their case without providing any new material at that stage. Scholes appeared to be a similar age to their own barrister, Roger Galbraith. He had the same air of easy confidence. This, and the fact that he was a fellow member of Lincoln's Inn, had studied law at Oxford, as had Galbraith, and the fact that they were regularly opponents in court, added to the impression, for Anne and Kevin at least, that this was indeed a great game in which, for Scholes and Galbraith, the game itself was the thing that mattered, and not the issues at stake.

When the hearing was adjourned, Anne and Kevin made their way to Tavistock Square to visit Emma in the Infirmary before returning to Didcot. They broke their journey to call in at the hotel at Heathrow where Sandor normally stayed, as he was expected to arrive in London that evening. He had just arrived but was tired after the flight from Budapest, so they only stayed for a short while. As ever, they were pleased to see him – especially Anne.

The first full day of the hearing was allocated to counsel for the plaintiffs to present their case. Clifford Scholes was eloquent and in good form.

"It's very natural that we should feel the deepest sympathy with the defendants in this case. To discover that their child, their first and so far, their only child, has an incurable condition that will lead inevitably to the child's early death must be one of the most devastating things that can happen to young parents, such as Kevin and Anne Norton.

"Which of us who are parents cannot immediately identify with their plight? In such a desperate situation, it is only too readily understandable that, as parents, they would seek any remedy that might save their child from what harsh nature has ordained, however improbable, fantastic or far-fetched that remedy might be. In these circumstances, they become vulnerable to those who might exploit them for their own purposes, taking advantage of their desperation. Powerful emotions are involved – perhaps the most powerful of emotions – but powerful emotions are not always the best guide to doing what is right, and we must never lose sight of that most supreme calling of the law: to do what is right. That is the ultimate responsibility of this court: to do what is right. Where a child is involved, as in this case, to do what is right is to do what is in the best interests of the child when all factors have been taken into consideration, however turbulent the emotions involved. The witnesses I will be calling will make it very clear that the plaintiffs have the best interests of Emma Norton as their objective, despite all the emotion surrounding this case."

The first witness for the plaintiffs called by Scholes was the senior administrator at the National Children's Infirmary, Brett Morrison. Morrison launched into a prepared speech about the National Children's Infirmary, extolling its reputation as one of the country's leading institutions in the field of paediatrics. It was, he said, a reputation that rested on a history of sound judgements, based on well-established medical practices and knowledge, and not on unproven and risky experiments, and unauthorised treatments and drugs which had not passed proper testing procedures. No one, he said, had greater empathy and understanding of the way the Nortons must be feeling in this tragic situation than he did. Everyone present would understand and sympathise with the awful situation they faced, especially those who were parents themselves.

But however great the sympathy and the emotions involved, it was essential not to lose sight of the importance of basing decisions on well-established medical practices and knowledge, and not risking prolonging the pain and suffering of an innocent child in order to experiment with unproven and unauthorised treatments and drugs. Even the Nortons, he said, would come to understand and accept the wisdom of that in the fullness of time. That was the issue at the heart of this case.

Cross-examination of the witness by the defence was brief.

"Are you a doctor, Mr Morrison?" Roger Galbraith asked.

"I'm the senior administrator at the National Children's Infirmary," Morrison bristled defensively.

"That doesn't answer my question. Are you a doctor?"

"I've already explained my office and responsibilities," Morrison retorted brusquely.

"That doesn't answer my question, which is: are you a doctor, or do you have any medical qualifications of any kind? A simple 'yes' or 'no' will suffice."

Clifford Scholes rose to ask the judge for the question to be disallowed. The judge, Mr Justice Robertson, ruled that the question should be answered. Directed to answer the question, Morrison admitted that he was not a doctor. Roger Galbraith then followed up his question with another.

"And have any of the medical staff at your infirmary ever published any research on Behrens-Hillingdon Syndrome?"

Morrison frowned.

"I'm not in a position to answer that."

"Let me rephrase the question. Knowing that this case was coming up, and knowing that Behrens-Hillingdon Syndrome would be a prominent issue in the case, can you cite one piece of research into Behrens-Hillingdon Syndrome published by any of the medical staff at your infirmary?"

"I ... don't have the information to answer that question."

"It's a simple enough question. Can you cite just one piece of research into Behrens-Hillingdon published by any of the medical staff at your infirmary? A simple 'yes' or 'no' will suffice."

Scholes again appealed against the question, again unsuccessfully. Morrison then grudgingly admitted that he could not cite any such research.

"No further questions," Roger Galbraith said.

The second witness for the plaintiffs was the consultant in charge of Emma Norton's case, Dr Bahadur Choudhry. Dr Choudhry began by introducing himself and explaining his academic background, qualifications and experience, and his role at the Infirmary. He was, he said, privileged to work at such a prestigious institution, which had given him wide-ranging experience in the treatment of seriously ill children over many years. In consequence, that meant that he was now one of the most experienced paediatricians in the country, as would be acknowledged by any reputable medical authority.

Like Morrison, he fully understood the plight the Nortons were in as parents of Emma, and he felt only the deepest sympathy for them. These feelings, however, only made him more determined to do what was right, which meant what was in the best interests of the child. Since Behrens-Hillingdon Syndrome was incurable, with an inevitable outcome, and since there were no treatments proven to have any effect, it would simply be cruel to prolong the child's suffering in the forlorn hope that such a treatment might become available. He realised that it would always be very hard for any parents to accept this truth, but as a clinician, it was incumbent on him not to lose sight of it, and the fact that prolonging the child's suffering to no purpose was detrimental to her best interests. As an expert witness, his main concern was to impress the importance of this last point on the court.

Cross-examining the witness, Roger Galbraith quickly came to the point.

"Dr Choudhry, can you advise the court what research you have undertaken and published, in a professional capacity, either individually or jointly, into Behrens-Hillingdon Syndrome?"

"What matters most in a situation like this is breadth of experience in treating a whole range of paediatric conditions, and the wider problems, including moral and ethical issues, associated with them," Choudhry replied. "There are few clinicians in the country who can match the breadth of such experience that I have."

"I'm afraid that doesn't answer my question. Have you, either individually or jointly, published any research into Behrens-Hillingdon Syndrome?"

"As a paediatrician, I have experience of treating children with a number of very rare conditions. The fact that I may not have published research into a particular condition does not detract from my wider competence, based on experience, in dealing with such conditions."

"Understanding very rare conditions such as Behrens-Hillingdon inevitably involves the specialist knowledge associated with research, especially research into how such conditions might be treated. That has always been the case in the history of medicine, as I'm sure you are aware. Have you published any such research into Behrens-Hillingdon Syndrome, Dr Choudhry?"

Dr Choudhry finally admitted that he had not.

"Have any of the medical staff at the National Children's Infirmary published any research into Behrens-Hillingdon Syndrome?" Roger Galbraith asked.

"I don't have information to hand about all the research published by all the medical staff at the Infirmary."

"Well, let me rephrase the question. Can you cite just one piece of research into Behrens-Hillingdon Syndrome by any of the medical staff at the Infirmary?"

After some further prevarication, Choudhry admitted that he could not.

"No further questions," Roger Galbraith said briefly, glancing at the judge.

7

The following day was allocated to the defendants, for them to present their case. Once proceedings were under way, Roger Galbraith called Dr Sandor Zentai to the witness stand, giving the court a brief introduction.

Sandor began by introducing himself in more detail, describing his qualifications, career and current position at the Hungarian Institute of Medical Research in Budapest, specialisms and a general overview of his medical research. He then went on to describe his research into Behrens-Hillingdon Syndrome in some detail, including technical details, couched in layman's terms as far as possible.

He had begun his investigations with an analysis of the genetic basis of Behrens-Hillingdon Syndrome, identifying those parts of the genetic code that were responsible for the condition. Having codified the genes involved, he then shifted his focus onto methods of correcting or dealing with the genetic defects. This eventually led him to research the technique developed by Karyagin and Patolichev, on which the treatment he had developed was based. His research had confirmed that the Karyagin-Patolichev technique was basically sound, and also that it could safely be applied in the procedures he had developed for treating Behrens-Hillingdon Syndrome. Laboratory trials consistently indicated that the treatment he was developing successfully restored the defective DNA which was the cause of Behrens-Hillingdon Syndrome.

He had conducted this research over a period of several years, to be sure of his findings. During this time, he had regularly published his research findings in both Hungarian and international medical journals. This body of published research meant that he was now one of the world's foremost authorities on Behrens-Hillingdon Syndrome. One consequence of this was that, from time to time, he would be contacted about particular cases of the condition, usually by the parents of the child concerned. This was how Anne and Kevin Norton had first made contact with him. These contacts were infrequent because cases of Behrens-Hillingdon were rare, but those that had occurred had highlighted a similar range of problems facing those whose children were being treated for the condition.

These problems related to institutional attitudes towards the care of such children and, in particular, institutional attitudes towards the rights of parents in relation to the care of their children. Children suffering from Behrens-Hillingdon Syndrome were usually in institutional care from an early stage in the condition. Hitherto, there had been no known cure for this condition, and conventional practice in such situations was that the kindest thing to do was to minimise the child's suffering by ending life support and allowing the child to die.

In bureaucratic institutions there was a tendency for such perceptions to become embedded in the culture of the institution, despite the possibility that research might develop new treatments that could change the outlook for such conditions. This was especially true if such research was carried out at a rival institution, or in another country. It engendered a mentality of hubris in which the values of the institution, rather than the best interests of the patient, became paramount. It was, Sandor said, something he had had to face on several occasions, and it was this closed-minded attitude that Anne and Kevin Norton had faced from almost as soon as their child had been transferred to the National Children's Infirmary. A decision had been made that there was no possibility of a cure for Behrens-Hillingdon, and that was that.

However, this closed-mindedness was reinforced and, indeed, only made possible at all, by the attitude of the government and state authorities. In many countries, including Britain, the official view was that all children were the exclusive property of the state, and that the right to decide the fate of any child, up to and including ending the child's life, lay exclusively with the state, regardless of the wishes or views of the child's parents. Since this was the official view in Britain, Sandor appealed to the judge, as the person who now embodied this official right in the case of this child, Emma Norton, to acknowledge that the treatment which he, Sandor Zentai, had developed for Behrens-Hillingdon Syndrome offered the possibility of a cure and that, therefore, the child's parents should be allowed to choose to have Emma receive the treatment to give her the chance of life.

With that appeal, Sandor ended his statement.

Clifford Scholes was immediately on his feet.

"Dr Zentai, isn't it true that your treatment for Behrens-Hillingdon Syndrome caused the death of a child in Nicaragua not long ago?"

"No, it is not true," Sandor replied impassively.

"But I have here a copy of the child's death certificate," Scholes exclaimed triumphantly, waving the document about, "which clearly states that your treatment was a contributory cause of the child's death. If that is the case, it undermines the whole basis of the defendants' case against the plaintiffs."

"It is not the case," said Sandor. "The child died of MRSA, being already severely weakened by Behrens-Hillingdon Syndrome. Several other children on the same ward died of MRSA in the same outbreak. The child had not been receiving my treatment for long enough for it to have had any significant effect on his metabolism, either positive or negative. I, too, have a copy of the death certificate you refer to – sent to me by the doctor who wrote it. He was the doctor on the ward in the hospital in Nicaragua where this happened."

Sandor produced the document as he was speaking. He continued:

"This was to ensure that I had evidence of what had actually taken place. When the doctor wrote out the death certificate, he made no mention of my treatment as a possible cause of death. His conclusion was that the child had died of MRSA, being already seriously weakened by Behrens-Hillingdon. That was what he wrote on the certificate. It was only subsequently that the certificate was amended to include a reference to my treatment. This was done by the hospital administrator at the hospital in Nicaragua where these events happened. It was done without the knowledge or approval of the doctor who had made out the certificate. As you can see on this copy, the reference to my treatment is in a different handwriting from the rest of the certificate. The hospital administrator was not a doctor, but merely a bureaucrat with no medical qualifications of any kind. This was also confirmed by the doctor who made out the certificate. The doctor made a formal complaint about the matter, but evidently the hospital administrator had friends in the right places, and no action was taken. The doctor sent me a copy of the affidavit he made out, as evidence that the amendment to the death certificate was unauthorised and of no medical validity. I have a copy of his affidavit here."

Clifford Scholes was on his feet to intervene at this point.

"Dr Zentai, all this is of doubtful relevance to the matter at hand. The individual you're referring to isn't present to be questioned by this court, and an unsupported affidavit can hardly stand against an official document such as a death certificate, which in this case clearly states that your treatment was a possible contributory cause of this child's death. On the basis of this information, and particularly on the basis of the relevant official document, my clients are fully justified in taking the view that your treatment does not offer any viable alternative course of action. Their position is entirely justified."

"Your premise appears to be that official documents can never be falsified," Sandor retorted. "This one has been, and I have the evidence to prove it."

"Since the individual you refer to is not here to be cross-questioned, your evidence remains unsubstantiated," Clifford Scholes replied. Turning to the judge, he said: "No further questions."

Roger Galbraith did his best to retrieve the situation.

"Since the evidence in relation to this matter is available here for inspection, I must request that the court examines it." He took the documents from Sandor and handed them to the judge.

"The handwriting of the letter is clearly the same as the handwriting on the certificate – except for this line here on the certificate under the section headed '*Causas contributivas de muerte*', referring to Dr Zentai's treatment, which is in quite a different hand. As Dr Gonzalez explains in the letter, this addition was not authorised by him, and is therefore not a valid part of the certificate. The reference on the certificate by Dr Gonzalez to Dr Zentai's treatment is here, under a separate section headed '*Información adicional*'. The signatures on the two documents are also the same."

The judge nodded, then instructed the Clerk of the Court to record that he had examined the documents.

There being no further witnesses to call, the sitting was adjourned by the judge.

The court sitting was resumed that afternoon, for the judge to deliver his summary and decision. The judge began with a résumé of the case and the situation leading up to it. He went on to explain that in coming to his decision, he had taken into account not just the evidence and arguments presented by the plaintiffs and the defendants but also legal precedent from similar cases in the recent past, as well as law relating to children in general. In particular, he said, the fact that this case was taking place at all emphasised the principle, essential in his view, that it was the state that had the final right to make decisions about children, over and above any claims by parents or families. Taking all these factors into consideration, he had no doubts about his decision to find in favour of the plaintiffs on all counts. As one of the country's leading institutions in the field of paediatrics, he found that they had a clearly superior claim to have the best interests of the child as their priority, set against the unproven claims of Dr Zentai, over which serious questions remained. He therefore granted the plaintiffs the power to appoint a guardian *in loco parentis*, replacing Kevin and Anne Norton in that role, and thereafter to take whatever action they felt would be in the best interests of the child, including ending life support, if they decided that that was the best thing to do. As per legal precedent, he would allow the defendants to appeal and, if they did, no action should be taken by the plaintiffs in the matter while an appeal was pending, but in his view, it would be in the best interests of the child if the defendants did not prolong the child's suffering by appealing.

An anguished cry of, "Nooooo!" from Anne was obscured by the sounds of the court rising for the judge as he made his exit from the courtroom. The court ushers moved forwards to accompany the various parties from the courtroom. They were used to seeing emotion in these situations.

Anne and Kevin, Sandor Zentai and Roger Galbraith assembled briefly in the lobby. Anne was crying uncontrollably, and Kevin could not comfort her. Sandor took control of the situation. He turned to Roger Galbraith.

"Is there a side entrance I can bring a taxi to?"

Roger Galbraith pointed.

"Through those doors, then keep going until you reach the side door to the street. Turn left and walk down to the gates. Tell the taxi to come to the side entrance gates."

"Anne and Kevin are in no state to face people. There are quite a few people outside the front entrance, demonstrating in support of them. Could you go and speak to them? Explain what's happened and tell them that we're going to appeal."

Roger Galbraith nodded and made his way towards the main entrance. Sandor made a phone call and spoke to someone briefly. He then made another phone call to direct their taxi to the side entrance gates.

Sandor turned to face Anne, who was still crying. He held her gently by the arms.

"Don't despair," he said. "This was expected. It's time for Plan B. There's someone I need you to meet."

A few minutes later, they were climbing into the taxi at the side entrance gates. The taxi took them, not to Sandor's hotel, but on a much shorter ride to a hotel on Southampton Row. From the hotel lobby, they took the lift to the second floor, where Sandor led them to the door of room 211 and tapped lightly on the door. The door was opened by a man whom Anne realised she had seen before but, in her current state, couldn't immediately remember his name.

"Come in," the man said. He bade them all sit down.

"I know you ..." Anne said.

"Yes, we've met before. Dr Peter Jones, from UCLA. I accompanied Sandor on one or two of his visits to examine Emma at the National Children's Infirmary. I understand very well that this is a very traumatic moment for you, given what's just happened. The judge has just confirmed that your little girl, Emma, is being held hostage by the British state, which intends to use its power to end her life. There'll be an appeal against the judgement, but appeals take time, and Emma doesn't have that time. There needs to be action now to save her. That's the reason I'm here. Peter Jones isn't my real name. I'm not a doctor, and I have no connection with UCLA. I'm not a biochemist, and I'm not a specialist in human cell biology. I am a specialist in a much rarer profession: hostage rescue. Sandor will have told you about Plan B. Plan B is to rescue Emma from being held hostage by the British state, and to take her to a clinic in a safe location, beyond the reach of the British state, where she can receive the treatment that will give her a chance of life. The reason I'm here is to set up and carry out Plan B. All the preparations are now complete. The legal appeal is just to make them think that we're playing along with their game. The reality is that we're ready to go ahead with Plan B in the next few days. In a few days' time, Emma can be out of that place and safely in a clinic where she can receive Sandor's treatment. Are you with us?"

Anne felt a surge of emotion. She suddenly realised who this man reminded her of.

"Yes," she answered. "Yes, oh yes!"

8

Vernon Mitchell turned and walked over to his desk on hearing the discreet purring tone of the internal intercom phone.

"Your visitor has arrived, Mr Mitchell," his secretary informed him.

"OK, Liz. Can you have him brought through?"

Vernon Mitchell's ranch, Maple Ridge, was built on the summit of a gentle rise in the centre of a five hundred-acre estate in the lush, rolling parkland of Kentucky's Bluegrass country. Mitchell had begun his business career as a property developer, and had become a millionaire by the time he was thirty. However, it was trading on the international foreign exchange markets which had made him a billionaire, and he was now one of America's wealthiest men.

In many ways, Vernon Mitchell was a man out of his time. Traditional Christian beliefs had led to him having equally traditional conservative political views, in sharp contrast to the great majority of the wealthy elites. He used his wealth to support conservative political causes, both at a political level and more generally, such as supporting individuals in legal cases, both in the United States and elsewhere. In particular, he had a suspicious and negative view of the power of the state, regarding all government as inherently bad, as did most traditional conservatives, and seeing any government powers beyond the minimum required by the Constitution as excessive and unwarranted.

He especially valued the principle of individual liberty and despised what he regarded as socialist bureaucracies because of their threat to individual liberty. It was these qualities that had led to his involvement in the Emma Norton case. This had come about as a result of a chance conversation. Mitchell had been attending a Christian convention in Texas. He had got into conversation with one of the delegates, who happened to be a doctor. The conversation had turned to politics and philosophy, and Vernon Mitchell had explained his views about the excessive power of the state in most countries, citing as an example the way life support of critically ill people could be turned off by the state against the wishes of their relatives, even when possible alternative treatments were available.

"It's interesting you should say that," the doctor had replied. "I know a doctor in Europe personally who has developed a new treatment for a rare condition and who has repeatedly been prevented from using it to try to save the lives of patients – in this case babies and infants – because of the attitude of authorities determined to use the power of the state to switch off life support systems because they have decided they don't want the child to live."

He was referring to Sandor Zentai, and he had gone on to explain the situation Sandor faced, quoting some of the case histories. Vernon Mitchell was immediately interested. He had asked for more details and, finally, if he could be put in touch with Sandor. This had duly been arranged. Extensive correspondence by email established that they had a strong mutual interest with regard to the work that Sandor was doing.

Mitchell and Zentai had eventually met in Vienna, during a business trip Mitchell was making to Europe. Several long conversations over a period of two days had resulted in an agreement about the courses of action they would take in the event of another case where state or other bureaucratic officialdom prevented Sandor's treatment being given to a child with Behrens-Hillingdon Syndrome, despite the wishes of the parents. They agreed on secure means of communication so that they could contact each other whenever necessary. For Vernon Mitchell, this was a cause he could support with wholehearted enthusiasm, not just for the sake of the child concerned but also as a means of thwarting a system and an ideology which he despised. For Sandor Zentai, it was an assurance that next time – and he was sure there would be a next time – the outcome was going to be different.

This had been the situation when Sandor had received the first email from Anne and Kevin Norton. He had advised Vernon Mitchell, and once it had become clear that the circumstances surrounding this case were following the same pattern as in previous cases, they agreed to initiate the procedures they had discussed and planned. Sandor had forwarded to Mitchell an image of Emma, taken on his mobile phone during his first visit to the National Children's Infirmary to see her. It showed Emma looking up from her cot, her blue eyes wide open and curious. Vernon Mitchell had gazed at the image for a long time.

A discreet knock on the door heralded the arrival of Mitchell's visitor, as his secretary, Liz, ushered him in.

"Mr John Roberts to see you, Mr Mitchell," she announced.

Roberts and Mitchell shook hands and, at Mitchell's suggestion they made their way out to the end of the terrace behind the ranch house. A table and chairs had been set up at a spot that commanded a splendid view of the estate. More importantly, it was a place where they could talk with no risk of being overheard. As recorded in Mitchell's office diary, his visitor, John Roberts, was an investment analyst. His credentials included extensive experience in currency and futures trading, and his consultancy offered a wide range of financial services.

In fact, 'John Roberts' had no experience whatsoever in financial services; his 'consultancy' was an entirely fictitious creation; and his name was not John Roberts. His real name was Travis Powers. He was a consultant, but in a very different kind of business. Over a number of years, he had established a formidable track record in covert operations against terrorists, criminals and other agencies in cases where hostages had been taken and were being used for blackmail or held for ransom. Hostage rescue was a profession that required special qualities: physical toughness; astute intelligence and the ability to assess difficult situations very rapidly; immense self-confidence; but above all, the motivation to do a job that was often dangerous, and sometimes extremely dangerous. For Travis Powers, the central motivation was a desire to combat those who malevolently used force, or the power behind force, against people who were essentially helpless victims, whether for monetary gain, or to exult in a demonstration of their power.

This quality had been recognised by Vernon Mitchell, reflecting his own values, and had led to him deciding to entrust Travis Powers with this mission. From conversations held during a number of meetings, it had become clear to Mitchell that Travis Powers was exactly the man he needed for the kind of job he had in mind. In particular, this related to the fact that Travis was prepared to act against government and state agencies if necessary.

At a time when governments were becoming increasingly corrupt and totalitarian under the influence of Globalism, they were thereby losing any moral right to be treated any differently from criminal organisations. All of this necessitated Travis undertaking very detailed and elaborate security procedures. This included the extensive use of aliases in order to protect his real identity. Having access to sophisticated technology, Travis had developed the facilities to create completely new identities, backed up with full documentation, both physical and digital. He was able to create a new identity for almost any role he needed to adopt for the particular job in hand. He also created aliases for the members of his team and, where necessary, he could create completely new identities for the victims he rescued, to allow them to start new lives free from past events. He was using one such alias at that moment – that of 'John Roberts, Investment Analyst'. This was primarily to protect Vernon Mitchell, allowing him to claim that he had never met, nor ever had anything to do with, Travis Powers, or the kind of business that Travis was engaged in. Face-to-face meetings also had particular advantages in times when there were no longer any moral certainties.

As this was the final meeting between Vernon Mitchell and Travis Powers before the operation went ahead, they had much to discuss. In this operation, Mitchell was providing the money and the means; Travis was providing the plan and the personnel. Integrating these so that the plan worked as intended, while maximising personal security for all those involved, meant discussing a lot of detail. By the end of the conversation, when all the many details to be decided upon had been agreed, Vernon Mitchell felt more than reassured by his impression of Travis's capabilities and competence. It wasn't often that one came across such a combination of absolute self-assurance, competence and single-mindedness of purpose. Mitchell was extremely confident that, on this mission, they were going to succeed.

9

Shortly before 10.00, a white Mercedes van turned off the A27 Shoreham bypass onto the access road to Shoreham airport, just west of Brighton. Following the long perimeter road brought the van down to the south side of the airfield and the main entrance to the airport. After checking in with airport security and being given clearance to go airside, the driver took the van round to the airside gate for vehicles, where the gate was opened for him by a security guard. The guard leaned in through the van's window to give the driver directions.

Once through the gate, the driver turned left onto the ramp and drove slowly past the row of hangars and warehouses along the south side of the ramp. Towards the far end of the ramp, he saw what he was looking for: on a concrete hardstand just off the ramp, a helicopter was parked – a Bell 222U, with a French registration. A man was standing beside the helicopter, evidently looking out for the van. Having identified the van, the man waved and indicated to the driver that he should bring the van up to the helicopter.

The driver turned off the ramp onto the hardstand and parked alongside the aircraft. The van and its driver were from Horsham Medical Instruments Ltd, a supplier of specialist equipment for hospitals. The driver's delivery schedule was normally to hospitals, clinics and GP surgeries, care homes, universities and colleges, and sometimes to private residences. This delivery was certainly out of the ordinary. He wouldn't have expected to be delivering to an airport. Deliveries of equipment to overseas locations were normally by specialist courier.

The man who greeted the driver was Sandor Zentai. It was he who had ordered the equipment that was being delivered, using an alias which had been created for him by Travis Powers. After checking through the consignment schedule and signing for the delivery, he helped the driver to unload the consignment and transfer it to the aircraft. The helicopter's pilot came through from the cockpit to supervise the loading. The smaller boxes fitted into the luggage compartment. Two larger boxes went into the helicopter's passenger cabin, each being secured behind one of the seats.

After the van had departed, the helicopter pilot, Keith Brown, walked slowly round the aircraft, checking that it was ready for flight. As the aircraft's pilot, Keith Brown worked for Vernon Mitchell. He was one of three pilots on Mitchell's regular staff. He was a very experienced helicopter pilot, and Mitchell had commissioned him to select and acquire the helicopter to be used for this job. The specific nature of the job meant that there were fairly exacting technical requirements for the aircraft involved. Keith Brown supplied the technical expertise; Vernon

Mitchell supplied the finance for whatever he decided was required.

With the inspection complete, they both climbed aboard the aircraft. Sandor sat beside Keith Brown in the cockpit. Brown went through the cockpit checklist before starting the engines, listening to each engine spooling up as he watched the rev counters. Once the engines had reached idling speed, Keith Brown listened to them for a minute before completing the cockpit checks. He then contacted the tower to request clearance for take-off, referring to the flight plan he had filed with air traffic control. There was a short pause before the tower advised course and altitude details and told him to 'stand by'. Sandor, sitting beside Keith Brown, was wearing headphones and could also hear the conversation. For Sandor, it was a novel experience to be sitting in the cockpit of an aircraft. A few minutes later, clearance for take-off came through from the tower. After a final series of checks, Keith Brown gradually opened the throttle. The whine of the engines rose in pitch as they spooled up to maximum power. Once he was satisfied that the engines were running smoothly, he moved the pitch control until the rotor blades took effect. The helicopter lifted off the hardstand, moving forwards as it did so.

As the aircraft climbed, Keith Brown turned east and then south. Once clear of the airport, they crossed the railway bridge over the river and the A259 coast road. After crossing the coast at about five hundred feet, they climbed steadily as they flew out over the English Channel. At a thousand feet, Keith Brown levelled off, on a bearing of 158 degrees. A few minutes later, he made contact with French air traffic control, to confirm details of course and altitude.

They crossed the French coast near Fécamp, with the land starting abruptly in high, white cliffs. A couple of minutes after crossing the coast they passed over a large river – the Seine – before continuing south-south-east across the French countryside. Sandor found that flying at such a low altitude made the journey much more interesting than it would have been in a high-flying jet, with buildings, traffic and even people being clearly visible.

As they were crossing forty-nine degrees north, Keith checked with air traffic control and put the aircraft into a long, steady climb in order to clear the Massif Central, which lay ahead. Beyond the River Loire, which they crossed a few miles west of Orléans, the landscape changed suddenly from farmland to forest, the forest extending for a huge distance. Farmland returned south of Vierzon, but once they had passed Montluçon, the landscape became more upland in character, with smaller fields and winding, forested river valleys. The sun gleamed from small lakes which dotted the countryside. A few miles west of Clermont-Ferrand they flew over the distinctive truncated cones and craters of the Puy-de-Dôme, the now-extinct volcanoes largely covered in forest. Further south, the country became more alpine, with a succession of long, winding mountain ridges, mostly forest-covered, enclosing numerous secluded valleys, some containing villages and the occasional small town; others, higher up, empty of human habitation. The mountains and hills continued more or less right down to the coast, but by the time they could see the Mediterranean ahead, many of the wide valleys were filled with the ordered rows of vineyards between the darker green of woods and forest.

Shortly before reaching the coast, Keith spoke with air traffic control to confirm details of their position, route and destination. They crossed the coast near Montpellier, the coast itself here being formed by a long, narrow spit of land, behind which lay a series of coastal lagoons. They flew steadily out to sea, gradually losing height as they did so. Near to the coast, the sea was dotted with numerous small pleasure craft, with powerboats leaving long, white wakes behind them. At length, their destination came into sight: a much larger vessel, moving slowly parallel to the coast. Keith was already in radio contact with the vessel as they approached it. The MV *Aegiale* was a sixty-five metre yacht owned by Vernon Mitchell and kept, for most of the year, at its mooring in the yacht basin in Monaco harbour. For the previous twenty-four hours, *Aegiale* had been cruising off the French coast, in preparation for this rendezvous. On receipt of a text message from Keith Brown, *Aegiale* had stood in towards the coast and taken up station just outside the twelve nautical-mile limit of French territorial waters.

As the helicopter approached, the yacht slowed and came to a stop in the water, with its propellers turning just enough to counteract drift in the current. With *Aegiale* now almost motionless riding a gentle ocean swell, Keith brought the helicopter in to land on the large letter 'H' in the centre of the helipad, set high up on the yacht's stern. As the engines died and the rotors slowed to a stop, Sandor unfastened his seatbelt and removed his headphones while Keith completed the final cockpit checks on landing. Opening the cockpit door, Sandor stepped out into bright sunlight and took a deep breath of warm, Mediterranean sea air. Waiting to greet them were Vernon Mitchell and his wife, Barbara. Barbara had said, once she had heard about Emma's case, that wild horses would not have prevented her from being there.

With the assistance of members of the yacht's crew, the boxes of equipment loaded onto the helicopter at Shoreham were carried down to the yacht's sick-bay. *Aegiale* had a small, but well-equipped, sick-bay, suitable for non-specialist general care. Under Sandor's guidance, Vernon Mitchell had upgraded all the sick-bay's general facilities as much as possible. With the new equipment, Sandor was now transforming it into a specialist intensive care unit. At least one further flight would be needed in order to bring in everything that Sandor required.

And beyond that, these flights also served another purpose …

10

The final items that had been ordered from Horsham Medical Instruments Ltd weren't delivered to Shoreham airport but were collected from the company's premises in Horsham. The driver of the plain white Ford delivery van that collected them was Travis Powers, using one of his many aliases. After completing the consignment paperwork, Travis was assisted by two company employees in loading the equipment into the van and securing it. This included the largest of the items ordered by Sandor Zentai, and one of the most important: a baby transport incubator.

From Horsham, Travis took the A24 north into London. Driving into central London along Kennington Park Road, he crossed the river via Waterloo Bridge into Westminster. A few minutes later, he turned off Tavistock Place onto Wakefield Street and stopped in front of a gated entranceway. Using a remote control, he opened the double metal gates, which swung inwards. Once through the gates, which closed automatically behind him, he drove down a ramp which led to an underground car park. On each side of a central space was a row of lock-up garages for rent. Using the remote control, Travis opened one of the garage doors and then parked the van in the garage. After checking that various items were ready for when they would be needed, he then locked the van, closed and locked the garage and walked back up to the street. He walked for a couple of hundred yards to a pub on Leigh Street, from where he phoned for a taxi. When it arrived, he directed the driver to take him to St John's Wood. Twenty minutes later, the taxi dropped him off on St John's Wood High Street. He paid the driver in cash for the fare. He walked up the High Street and turned into Charles Lane, walking past a long row of lock-up garages, some of which were to rent. He stopped in front of a garage which was fronted by a set of folding wooden doors. He tapped on the wicket gate set in the end door, tapping out his initials in Morse code, in a prearranged signal, and called out:

"It's me."

After a few moments, the wicket gate was opened by Charlie Taylor, who closed the gate again as soon as Powers had stepped inside. Charlie Taylor was one of Travis's team for this mission. One of his areas of expertise was vehicles, of almost any kind, as he demonstrated at that moment. Most of the garage was occupied by a white Mercedes delivery van, slightly larger than the Ford van that Travis had just driven up from Horsham, and, beside it, a small, silver-coloured Toyota saloon car. Both of the vans and the car were rented, from different car and van rental companies. At the back of the garage, upright on its stand, was a BMW motorcycle. Charlie had acquired the bike on the second-hand market. It was an ex-police bike which had been put up for disposal, so it was in an all-white finish. Since acquiring the bike, Charlie had been busy restoring the police markings and fittings which had been removed prior to disposal. These included flashing blue emergency lights fore and aft and a 'Police – Stop' illuminating sign on the back of the bike. He had more or less completed the job and was in the process of adding the finishing touches when Travis arrived.

Travis gazed at the bike admiringly. It was to be an important part of the plan. Now resplendent in its police markings, even a police officer wouldn't be able to tell that it wasn't the genuine article. Travis jokingly made a comment to that effect. When Charlie had completed the finishing touches, Travis helped him fasten a motorcycle cover over the bike. Charlie then opened the garage doors, got into the van and drove it out into the roadway. He got out and opened the van's rear doors. Travis helped him unload a long metal ramp, which they fixed to the back of the van. They then loaded the bike into the van, pushing it up the ramp. The bike was heavy, and it was hard work, but once it was in the back of the van, Charlie put it up on its stand and lashed it down. Jumping out, he slid the ramp back into the van, closed the rear doors and then reversed the van back into the garage. Another part of the plan was now ready to go.

They both climbed into the silver Toyota, which Charlie backed out into the street. Once the garage was secured and locked, Charlie drove Travis to his hotel on Southampton Row, before heading back to his own hotel in St John's Wood, which was within walking distance of

Charles Lane. He put the Toyota back into the garage and walked back to his hotel.

Back in his room at his hotel on Southampton Row, Travis switched on a small tablet which had been adapted for this job and logged into a special program which he had installed on the tablet. Using this program, he had been able to hack into the email system of the National Children's Infirmary, enabling him to read all the emails on the Infirmary's email system. This meant that for some time he had been reading all their emails relating to Emma Norton, both internal emails, emails to other parts of the NHS and the Department of Health, and, of particular interest, emails to and from the lawyers representing the Infirmary in the legal case against the Nortons. This information had proved invaluable in arranging the details, and especially the timing, of Plan B. Some of the emails made it clear that there was clandestine collaboration between the Infirmary's legal team and both the judge and the Ministry of Justice about the final outcome of the case, indicating that this was effectively a foregone conclusion. The appeal process was to be used to ensure that Emma's condition deteriorated beyond a point where any remedial treatment was possible, to bring about the outcome desired by both the Infirmary and the government. As well as copying the information, Travis was also passing it on, discreetly and indirectly, to Sandor Zentai and the Nortons.

Elsewhere in the Infirmary's email system, Travis had found something else of interest. From a perusal of the emails from the Infirmary's Supplies Department, he discovered that they obtained most of their medical equipment, including things like monitors and support systems, from a company called Allied Hospital Equipment Ltd of Woking. This meant that there were regular visits to the Infirmary by Allied Hospital Equipment's delivery vans to deliver equipment and collect equipment which needed servicing or repair. Allied Hospital Equipment's main premises were on an industrial estate on the north side of Woking, close to the main road north out of the town. The information given in these emails included not only delivery dates but even the approximate time of day when deliveries and collections were arranged, as well as details of the consignments. It was the discovery of this information which had enabled Travis to formulate one of the key stages of Plan B.

11

For Anne and Kevin, the last couple of weeks of their ordeal were the hardest to bear, and also the most tumultuous. The week leading up to the hearing at the Royal Courts of Justice were the most difficult and traumatic of their lives, and especially so for Anne. The levels of stress she had experienced had been off the scale. She had hardly been able to eat or sleep in the torment of worry. She had still dared to hope that, somehow, there might be justice. What drove both her hope and her fear was the knowledge that, without the treatment that she needed, Emma's weakened systems had only a very limited time before they gave out and her life was extinguished. Every little heartbeat was now precious, as it maintained the fragile thread of life that Emma still clung to. The thought that any time soon, one of those little, faltering heartbeats would be the last, and that she, as a mother, could only wait, unable to help her baby, tormented Anne's every waking moment. In such distress, she could barely function, sometimes being unable to focus her mind on the simplest of everyday tasks. She admired how Kevin had managed to carry on in his job as an electrician, knowing that he was experiencing the same levels of stress. Being more taciturn, Kevin was not able to express his emotions as openly as Anne. But his distress was just as great and, at night, when she clung to him, they would sometimes cry in each other's arms.

The court hearing itself was the hardest thing that either of them had ever had to face, especially for Anne. The stress was terrible because she still dared to hope. Through all the tortuous, petty legal point-scoring, she still dared to hope. The judge's final ruling was therefore devastating, both in its finality and in the casual way he dismissed the life of her child. It was like being punched in the stomach by a pile-driver. Suddenly, the worst, the very worst, had happened. The blow was so great that it broke her. It broke her mind and her spirit, and in that terrible moment, a great wail of despair had been forced from her. As if in a dream, she saw the look of smug satisfaction on Clifford Scholes' face as he registered his victory, as if he derived personal satisfaction from killing her baby. How could such creatures even exist?

At first, there was total and complete despair, because of what this would mean for Emma. The despair was a physical pain, which rent her insides; rent her very soul. Kevin tried to comfort her, but she knew that inside, he was being crushed by the same despair. Increasingly, there was also anger; rage against those who wanted to kill her baby. In the lobby, there was confusion, but she took little of it in, and nor did she care. Sandor Zentai was there, yet even he could not comfort her. However, what happened next would be indelibly etched on her mind. Sandor spoke with their barrister, Roger Galbraith, and then he turned to her and said: "There's someone I need you to meet." She just nodded, too distraught to speak. They left the building by a side entrance and walked down to the street, where they were met by a taxi. The journey was very brief, to a nearby hotel; the hotel lift to the second floor; and then a man …

Anne would never forget the moment when she understood who this man was. Not his name – she never knew his real name – but his character, his purpose. The moment when she knew that her initial instinct about this man had been correct. The moment when she understood that his real purpose was to bring life. It meant that, for Emma, this was to be a time to live.

The next few days were dramatic with tension, but now of a different kind. Peter Jones – the name the Nortons continued to know him by – told them that Plan B was ready to go immediately, as he had been coordinating its preparations with the timing of the court hearing. The court's ruling in favour of the National Children's Infirmary, which had just taken place, was effectively the trigger for Plan B to go into operation. For Anne and Kevin, this meant that they had to prepare for an immediate departure from their home without giving any outward signs that they were doing so. Secrecy was paramount. No one was to be told what they were going to do.

Peter Jones gave them detailed guidance about the things they needed to do, and when, and a secure means of contacting him. It was essential that they subordinated everything to the mission to rescue Emma and to get her, and also themselves, to the safe location which had been prepared for them. This included concerns about their jobs, and financial and income security. The man who was making Plan B possible would, if necessary, guarantee their financial security for as long as they needed it as part of his determination to ensure that Emma was rescued and would receive the treatment she was being denied by the British authorities. There would be only one opportunity to rescue Emma, so they had to be prepared to subordinate everything to that. These missions only succeeded through single-mindedness of purpose, focusing only on the job in hand. In the end, everything came back to that: the job in hand, the job in hand, only the job in hand.

In the ordinary course of events, such abrupt and drastic action would be too daunting even to contemplate. But when the life of their daughter was at stake, it changed their perspective on everything. What had seemed of paramount importance before now became secondary and expendable. Now there was a new perspective and a new horizon, and everything was transformed.

There was, in any case, little time for discussion. They had a lot to do and little time to do it in. For their possessions, they had to pack two medium-sized suitcases, one each, with the things that they valued most. The advice was not to fill them with clothes and things that could be replaced but with things like family photos and mementos of their lives – things that couldn't be replaced. And they didn't have much time to decide what to pack. Peter Jones advised that he would be sending one of his team, acting as a courier, to collect the suitcases, so that they would not be seen leaving their house carrying suitcases. For each item they chose, they had to decide whether they had room for it, knowing they might well never see it again otherwise.

The suitcases were collected the following morning by Graham Smith, driving the Mercedes van from the lock-up garage in St John's Wood. Charlie Taylor had marked the van on either side with temporary artwork which read: 'Express Delivery'. Graham Smith was one of Travis Powers' regular team, who had only just arrived in Britain to take part in this mission. His role in most missions was to provide back-up support and, where necessary, physical 'muscle'. This mission required an extra team member, so Graham's role was essential. He had booked into a hotel in St John's Wood, just across the street from the hotel where Charlie Taylor was staying so that they both had access to the lock-up garage on Charles Lane. As with other members of the team, he was using a fully documented alias – 'Graham Smith' was not his real name. Back in St John's Wood, Graham transferred the two suitcases to the boot of the Toyota saloon. Charlie then removed the temporary artwork on the van, which had served its purpose.

For Anne and Kevin, there were other preparations they had to make for a prolonged and possibly indefinite absence from their home. As well as making the house secure for a long period of absence, they needed to make arrangements for long-term care and maintenance of the house, their other belongings and assets and other interests. Both Anne's and Kevin's parents still lived nearby. After some discussion, it was decided to entrust these matters to all four parents jointly. All four had been very supportive, especially since the onset of Emma's illness, doing whatever they could to help, sometimes staying over at Anne and Kevin's house to do so. They advised Peter Jones (as they knew him), and he responded with a legal document which he had had drawn up for this situation on legal advice. As soon as Emma had been rescued, he would make arrangements for Anne and Kevin to contact their parents, explain what had happened and forward the legal document to them to enable them to do whatever they could to secure Anne and Kevin's interests.

Peter Jones advised that there was a high risk that the authorities would ride roughshod over their legal rights once they understood what had happened, so they had to be prepared for that. They should also advise their parents of that risk as well. He said that he suspected that if the behaviour of the authorities became egregious, 'The Boss', as their anonymous benefactor (Vernon Mitchell) was always referred to, might take a further interest in the matter. He was not a man to be crossed lightly.

Other arrangements also had to be made. For Kevin, leaving his job was no easy matter, even though saving the life of his daughter automatically took top priority. He had worked for Hatstons Engineering Ltd in Didcot for nearly ten years, including an apprenticeship with them as an electrician on leaving school. He enjoyed the job, which often involved trips to Hatstons' customers to service their equipment. Having a steady job with Hatstons had enabled him to make a start in life – to get married, to take out a mortgage to buy a house and to start a family. For Kevin, it was an emotional wrench to have to end his employment with Hatstons, and particularly to have to do it in such an abrupt way, with no notice or warning. Peter

Jones gave him some guidance about the wording of the letter of resignation he prepared, to try and mitigate the situation as far as was possible. The letter would only be posted once Emma had successfully been rescued.

For Anne, there were no such complications. She was still on maternity leave from her job at the local grocery store, so her absence wouldn't immediately be noticed there. She had enjoyed her job there, but in the scale of things, it counted for nothing against the chance to save the life of her daughter. She was ready.

12

On the Monday morning, Graham Smith left his hotel in St John's Wood at 6.00 to walk to the lock-up garage on Charles Lane. On this mission, timing was everything. The journey he was about to make had already been timed by Charlie Taylor in order to help plan the schedule for the day's events. All the journeys on this day's mission were interlinked, and although the plan had margins for error to allow for the unexpected, timing was still important.

Five minutes later, Graham reached the lock-up garage on Charles Lane. He went in by the wicket gate, which he closed behind him. After unlocking the Toyota, he sat in the driver's seat to carry out a couple of technical checks first. A short while later, he opened the garage doors fully, backed the Toyota saloon out and secured the garage again before setting off.

He turned right into St John's Wood High Street, then left into Circus Road, carrying on until he reached the junction with Maida Vale, where he turned left. He drove down to Bayswater Road via Edgware Road and

Sussex Gardens. There was some traffic build-up on Edgware Road, but he reached Bayswater Road within schedule. Graham was fairly familiar with London, but he had a satnav clipped to the dashboard giving directions and updated traffic information. From Holland Park Avenue, he turned onto Holland Road, then down to West Cromwell Road.

Traffic here was fairly heavy, and it was twenty-five minutes before he reached West Cromwell Road. From then on, he was travelling against the main flow of traffic for a Monday morning, and there were no further problems. Ten minutes later, he was on the M4, travelling west. He exited at Junction 4 for Heathrow and, after going round a double roundabout, he turned into the approach road to one of the airport hotels. He drew up opposite the main hotel entrance. Almost immediately, Sandor Zentai emerged from the entrance and came over to the car. Sandor checked the car's number plate, then got into the front passenger seat. They exchanged passwords to confirm each other's identity. They hadn't met previously, but Powers had shown each of them images of the other to aid identification. Neither of them spoke much. Graham had taken part in many missions as part of Powers' team, but he always felt the tension at the start of a mission. Sandor was also feeling tense, but in his case, that was tempered by something akin to exhilaration from a premonition that this time, he was going to succeed. This child was going to live!

A few minutes later, they were back on the M4 westbound. They reached Junction 13 at 7.25 and turned onto the A34 northbound. By 7.40 they had reached the junction for Didcot and were driving into the town. By 7.50, Graham was parking the Toyota on Hagbourne Road just near the junction with Church Street. They sat and waited. A few minutes later, Kevin Norton appeared at the end of Church Street and looked up and down Hagbourne Road. His attention quickly focused on the Toyota saloon, and he checked the number plate as he walked towards it. As Kevin walked along the pavement towards the car, he recognised Sandor sitting in the front passenger seat. Kevin got into the back of the car and greeted Sandor.

"Not sure if you know Graham," Sandor said, by way of introduction.

Kevin suddenly realised that he did.

"Oh, you're the guy who collected our suitcases."

Graham nodded.

"Your suitcases are in the back," he said.

Anne made a last quick tour of the house, to check that she hadn't missed anything. She had gone through her list more than once, but there might still be something she had overlooked. Despite having been very happy in this little terraced house on Church Street, she had no regrets. She could not contemplate continuing to live there without Emma, so if the house was part of the sacrifice for Emma, she had no problem with that. In the living room, her attention was caught by a favourite family photo which had been left on the mantelpiece. She had contemplated whether to include it in the suitcase she had packed but decided against it. It was too big, and she had other photos. Perhaps she could rescue it at this last minute? She could carry it in her hand ... She left it where it was. No regrets.

A minute later, she was slamming the front door behind her and checking that it was locked. She glanced up at the house as she closed the front garden gate. She might never see it again. But it was already in the past. This day was for the future. And for Emma ...

She walked to the end of Church Street and onto Hagbourne Road. A number of vehicles were parked on the street, but she saw someone waving from the window of a small silver-coloured car nearby. As she walked towards it, she recognised Sandor sitting in the front passenger seat. The waving arm belonged to Kevin, who moved over on the back seat as she climbed in. When Graham turned to greet Anne, she too recognised him as the 'delivery driver' who had collected their suitcases.

A few minutes later, they were back on the A34, this time southbound. By 8.20 they had reached Junction 13 on the M4. There were queues of traffic on the slip roads through the junction, and it was nearly 8.40 before they were actually on the M4. Traffic on the M4 eastbound was heavy, especially on the Reading bypass, with traffic slowing to a crawl or even stationary at times. By the time they reached Junction 10, where they exited the M4, it was almost 9.15. Progress was much better once they were on the A329, where the traffic was lighter.

By 9.55 they were driving round the northern outskirts of Woking. From Chobham Road they turned onto Victoria Way and then onto Boundary Road, from which they turned into an industrial estate. Graham parked the Toyota across the street from the entrance to one of the anonymous-looking industrial units. A sign by the entrance to the unit read: 'Allied Hospital Equipment Ltd,

Woking' with a phone number underneath. A number of vans with the company's name on the side of them were parked on the forecourt in front of the unit. Once they were parked, Graham and Sandor then carefully put on close-fitting rubber face masks in order to disguise their identities during the mission. They settled down to wait. Whilst they were waiting, Graham reached into his pocket and produced a small electronic device which claimed his attention for a few minutes. The device was a small radio transmitter. He placed it on the dashboard in front of him.

Just after 10.30, a man emerged from the building and walked over to one of the vans. The van's indicator lights flashed as the man unlocked it. The man climbed into the driver's seat, then got out again and walked round to the back of the van and opened the rear doors, before going back into the building. A minute later, he and a second man emerged carrying a large box, which they loaded into the back of the van. The second man went back into the building and returned carrying two smaller boxes, which he loaded into the van. The first man had meanwhile climbed into the driver's seat. The second man closed the rear doors and climbed into the cab beside the driver.

As soon as the van started to move, Graham started the engine of the Toyota. He reached out and pressed a button on the radio transmitter, which sent out a short, coded message. Graham followed the van at a discreet distance as it turned left out of the industrial estate onto Boundary Road, then Walton Road, then left again onto Monument Road. On Monument Road, the morning sunlight was dappled by the trees which overhung the road on both sides all the way up to the roundabout. On the Six Crossroads roundabout, as soon as Graham saw the van exiting the roundabout onto Chertsey Road, he pressed another button on the radio transmitter to send out another coded signal, before following the van onto Chertsey Road. This part of the plan had been successfully completed. The quarry was now as good as in the bag.

13

At 6.30 on the Monday morning, Charlie Taylor checked out of his hotel in St John's Wood, and walked along to the lock-up garage on Charles Lane. He went into the garage through the wicket gate, which he closed behind him. The Toyota was gone, having been driven away by Graham Smith half an hour earlier. That part of the plan was already under way.

Charlie unlocked the Mercedes van, opened the rear doors and climbed in. He went through a quick check to confirm that everything needed was present, before climbing out and closing the doors again, then climbing into the driver's seat. His attention focused on a small device which was fixed to the top of the dashboard. He switched the device on and pressed one of the buttons on it before climbing out to inspect the number plates on the van, front and back. These number plates were one of Charlie's specialities. Although they looked like ordinary number plates, they were actually LCD display units, able to display any combination of numbers and letters at the touch of a button. Some discreet information-gathering had collected the registration numbers of several Mercedes vans of the same type and colour. These had been programmed into the control device, and any of them could be displayed on the LCD number plates at the touch of a button on the device. Similar LCD number plates had been attached to the Ford van and the Toyota saloon. The BMW motorcycle had a simple false number plate attached.

With the LCD number plates displaying the desired registration, Charlie opened the garage doors fully and drove the van out into the lane. After closing and locking the garage doors, he set off, initially following the same route taken by Graham in the Toyota half an hour earlier, but continuing down Edgware Road to Marble Arch. Traffic was already significantly heavier than when Graham had passed through, and it was after 7.00 by the time Charlie reached Marble Arch. A few minutes later he was driving along Bayswater Road approaching Lancaster Gate underground station.

Travis Powers checked out of his hotel on Southampton Row at 6.30 on the Monday morning. From the hotel he walked down Southampton Row to Holborn underground station. Ten minutes later, he was on a train on the Central Line, travelling west. He got off at Lancaster Gate and, on reaching the street, walked along to the traffic lights, crossed the road and walked back to take up a position on the pavement opposite the underground station.

After waiting for about fifteen minutes, he saw the Mercedes van coming towards him. He stood right on the edge of the pavement and waved. Charlie slowed and stopped the van as he drew level, without pulling over. Travis opened the passenger door and quickly climbed in. There were the inevitable irate horns sounding behind them, but Charlie was stopped for less than ten seconds before they were under way again. The plan had made allowance for Charlie to circle round Hyde Park for another run down Bayswater Road if Travis had been late, so the timing was still good.

"Any problems?" Travis asked as he fastened his seatbelt.

"Nope. Graham's on his way, so everything's now up and running."

Travis nodded.

When they reached Chiswick on the Great West Road, they departed from Graham's route and took the A316 onto the M3. From the M3 they moved onto the M25, leaving at the next exit, Junction 11, for Woking. By 8.30 they were on the A320 passing through Ottershaw. South of Ottershaw, the road ran through lush woodland, with the woods closely lining the road on each side.

The traffic was heavy on the A320, especially northbound, so Charlie drove down to the Paragon roundabout in order to get onto the A320 northbound. Now going north, Charlie slowed as he approached the junction with Brox Road. He turned left here, into an entranceway opposite the junction. This gave access to the entrance to a house just off the road but also to a lane which ran through the woods parallel to the A320, separated from it by about twenty yards of trees and dense undergrowth. The trees and undergrowth effectively screened the lane from the road. Charlie turned right onto the lane and drove along the lane for a short distance before pulling well in to the side and stopping.

There had been no significant delays thus far, so they now had a bit of time in hand. Charlie had been thoughtful enough to pack some ready-made sandwiches and bottled soft drinks in the van, so they ate breakfast sitting in the van. Having finished, they then put on close-fitting rubber face masks to disguise their identities. The first thing they did on getting out of the van was to reconnoitre the lane to see if there were any problems. Although traffic on the nearby road was still heavy, the lane was quiet, with no one else in sight.

They walked down to the entrance to the lane opposite the junction with Brox Road on the A320 to check if there were any problems, and if any people were around. In the other direction, the lane ran north for about four hundred yards until it was crossed by another entranceway from the A320 to a house just off the road. This second entranceway also formed part of the plan. The lane curved gently, so that from the second entranceway the Mercedes van was not visible where they had left it parked. Beyond the second entranceway, the lane continued north for another three hundred yards, where it came to an end by being crossed by a boundary fence. The fence was the property boundary of another house which stood a short distance off the A320.

This house stood in the middle of extensive grounds, of which this fence was part of the boundary. The wood through which the lane ran continued beyond the boundary fence. The grounds of the house were well-wooded. A short distance beyond the boundary fence, within the grounds of the house, there was a brick-built garden shed. Travis had confirmed that it was a garden shed on an earlier reconnoitre of the place. The shed was at the edge of the wooded area, with the front of the shed facing the house, and with trees and bushes around the sides and back of the shed. The trees and bushes meant that one could approach the back of the shed without being visible from the house. What was of interest was that there was a door at each end of the shed. This shed formed part of the plan and was one of the reasons why this location had been chosen.

Cautiously, Travis climbed over the fence and made his way through the trees to the back of the shed, while Charlie remained by the fence. The back door of the shed was fastened by a hasp, secured by a padlock. Travis produced a screwdriver and removed all the screws holding the hasp to the door. On his previous visit, he had treated the screws to liberal squirts of WD40, so now they came out fairly easily. He removed the entire assembly, including the padlock, and placed it on the ground nearby. Opening the door, he had a quick look inside the shed before closing it again and making his way back to the fence where Charlie was waiting.

"Everything looks fine there," Travis commented briefly after he had climbed back over the fence.

They walked back down the lane to the van. They opened the rear doors of the van and climbed in. After taking the cover off the bike, Charlie checked the bike over and made one or two last-minute adjustments. They then slid the metal ramp out, fixed it in place and slowly unloaded the bike. After briefly starting the engine, the cover was replaced until just before the bike was to be used. The metal ramp was slid back into the van and the rear doors closed. Travis then donned the police motorcycle gear that had been brought for the job: boots, jacket, high-visibility yellow vest with 'POLICE' in white on dark blue on the back, a belt with attached equipment pouches and motorcycle gloves over the latex gloves he was already wearing. A motorcycle helmet with standard police markings was ready for him to put on at the last moment. With all preparations complete, they sat in the van to wait.

Shortly after 10.30, a small radio device which Travis had placed on the van's dashboard in front of him emitted a short beep. Travis picked the device up and looked at it. It was showing the first coded message from Graham.

"Right, this is it – they've set off," he said. He reached for the motorcycle helmet and put it on. They got out of the van and went to take the cover off the bike. Charlie bundled the cover into the back of the van, closed the doors and locked the van. Travis had pushed the bike off its stand, climbed onto the bike and started the engine. He eased the bike slowly forwards over the short distance down to the first entranceway to the A320, opposite the junction with Brox Road, with Charlie walking beside him. Travis positioned the bike in the entranceway where he had a clear view of the A320 in both directions. He produced the radio device from his pocket. A minute later, the device beeped again and displayed the second coded message from Graham.

"Right, they're coming this way. Here we go!"

The traffic on the road was much lighter now, with long spaces between vehicles. Charlie walked across the road and took up a position behind a tree on the far side of the road from where he could watch the northbound traffic. He used a small monocular to study the oncoming vehicles. Just over a minute later he shouted across:

"Here they come!"

Travis watched the Allied Hospital Equipment van as it approached. About two hundred yards behind it was a small car, which Charlie, through the monocular, had already identified as Graham's Toyota. As the van passed him, Travis pressed the switches for the bike's siren and blue lights and pulled out in pursuit of the van. Behind him, Graham was already slowing down to turn into the entranceway that Travis had just left. With the bike's phenomenal acceleration, Travis rapidly overtook the van. As he did so, he switched on the illuminated 'POLICE-STOP' sign mounted on the back of the bike. He slowed as he approached the second entranceway, noting from the view in his mirrors that the van was slowing also. He came to a stop just beyond the second entranceway, positioning the bike across the left-hand carriageway, front wheel towards the kerb. He turned and watched as the van slowed to a stop. With his left arm, he indicated that the van should turn into the second entranceway, which it did. He followed it in, indicating with his arm that the van should then turn right onto the lane. He went past the van onto the lane and then turned the bike across the lane to bring the van to a stop. He got off the bike, put it on its stand and walked over to the van.

"Can you both get out, please," he said crisply.

They did so. They were both young lads in their early twenties, and they were both looking worried. Out of the corner of his eye, Travis could see the Toyota arriving at the second entranceway from the lane to the south.

"Can you provide some identification?" Travis asked them. To the driver of the van, he added: "Can I see your driving licence if you have it with you?"

They both started fumbling for their wallets. By this point, Charlie (who had been picked up at the first entranceway) and Graham had got out of the Toyota and were approaching Travis and the two men. Sandor was following a short distance behind. Graham, who was in the lead, was holding a revolver in his hand.

"Stand very still where you are, you three, and put your hands up where I can see them," Graham said. "Don't even think about doing anything stupid." This last was addressed to Travis, who slowly put his hands up as instructed.

The two young lads, still disoriented by being stopped by the police, were slower to respond. Graham stood a short distance behind and to the left of Travis.

"Put your hands up where I can see them, and stand very still," Graham repeated. He pointed the revolver directly at the nearer of the two lads and pulled back the hammer of the revolver. It made a clearly audible click. That had the desired effect. The lad put his hands up quickly, followed by the other lad. As Graham held the two lads at gunpoint, they were approached from behind by Charlie and Sandor, who quickly clamped a heavy, padded mask over the mouth and nose of each of them. The masks were impregnated with a fast-acting anaesthetic which Sandor had access to as a doctor. The anaesthetic was tasteless and odourless, so the two lads were unsuspecting until they both suddenly passed out after a few seconds. Charlie and Sandor caught them and lowered them to the ground. Graham opened the rear doors of the Allied Hospital Equipment van and, after looking in, pushed the boxes that had been loaded there forwards to create some space. He and Charlie then lifted each of the lads into the back of the van. Graham walked over to the Toyota to get a reel of duct tape.

"Everything's going like clockwork so far," he said to Anne and Kevin, who were still in the car.

They nodded.

"Will ... those two be alright?" Anne asked uncertainly.

"Yes. The anaesthetic will last for about an hour before they start to come round. They'll be properly trussed up by then," Graham said, indicating the duct tape.

He walked back to the van and climbed in. After removing the loose tabards they wore with their company's name on the back, Graham proceeded carefully to tape up the two lads, with tape around their mouths, ankles and wrists, with their arms behind their backs. Whilst he was doing this, Charlie closed the rear doors, then reversed the van back to the second entranceway, where there was room to turn it round. Travis climbed into the passenger seat, and Charlie then reversed the van north along the lane up to where it was crossed by the boundary fence.

They got out and opened the rear doors to let Graham out. Travis climbed over the boundary fence and made his way through the trees to the garden shed. He went in through the back door and pulled out the wheelbarrow he had noted there earlier. He wheeled it back to the fence. Charlie and Graham lifted one of the now well-taped-up lads out of the van, over the fence and, with assistance from Travis, into the wheelbarrow. Charlie climbed over the fence and helped Travis to push the barrow back to the shed and then to carry the lad into the shed. A few minutes later, the second lad had been carried into the shed in the same way. On its final trip, the barrow was loaded with the boxes the van had been carrying, which were also placed in the shed.

Travis searched the two lads for their phones, which he put into his pocket after ensuring they were switched off. He also took their company identity badges. With the shed door closed, Travis produced his screwdriver and screwed the hasp, with its padlock, back onto the door. On their way back to the fence, Travis put the two phones into a plant pot and covered it with a piece of broken tile, recovered from the shed, and placed the plant pot under a bush.

Back in the van, Charlie drove them down to the second entranceway. Travis and Graham got out there. Charlie turned the van round and then reversed the van slowly on down the lane to where the Mercedes van was parked. Travis followed on the motorcycle. The first thing was to load the motorcycle back into the Mercedes van, where it was lashed down again and covered with the motorcycle cover. Travis divested himself of the police motorcycle gear, which was stowed in the back of the Mercedes van.

They then turned their attention to the Allied Hospital Equipment van. Firstly, Charlie located the van's vehicle tracking device and disabled it. He then retrieved a set of LCD display units from the Mercedes van and fitted them over the Allied Hospital Equipment van's number plates. The control device, which had been placed on the dashboard, had been programmed with several registration numbers of other vans of the same type and colour. He quickly tested the system to make sure that everything was working. The Allied Hospital Equipment Ltd markings on the sides and back of the van were covered with sheets of the plastic film that Charlie used for this purpose. With the sheets in place, the van now looked like just another anonymous white van.

With everything completed, Charlie climbed into the Allied Hospital Equipment van and drove back up to the second entranceway where the others were waiting in the Toyota saloon. Travis followed in the Mercedes van. They both stopped, got out and walked over to the Toyota for a brief consultation about the progress of the plan and the time schedule, before embarking on the next stage. Charlie then manoeuvred the Allied Hospital Equipment van so that Travis could get past in the Mercedes van. Travis turned onto the A320 northbound, with the other two vehicles following a short distance behind, heading for London.

14

At 12.15, Travis turned the Mercedes van onto Wakefield Street from Tavistock Place. He drove a short distance up the street and pulled into the side to wait for the others. The vehicles had become separated in the London traffic, which was intentional, to avoid them being recorded together by traffic cameras. Within the next few minutes, the other two vehicles also turned into Wakefield Street.

Travis then moved the Mercedes van forwards to the entrance to the underground car park. He opened the gates with the remote control and drove the van down to the bottom of the ramp, stopping at the bottom of the ramp. He got out and walked forwards to the entrance to the main parking area. Just inside and above the entrance was a security camera covering the main parking area. He reached up and placed a polythene bag over the camera. He then drove the van forwards into the main parking area until it was just past the garage that contained the Ford van. He got out, opened the garage door and walked back up the ramp to reopen the gates, which had closed again automatically, to let the other two vehicles in.

The next quarter of an hour was one of intensive activity. Charlie and Graham opened the rear doors of the Mercedes van and unloaded the motorcycle, which was wheeled into the garage. Travis had unlocked the Ford van so that Sandor could prepare the baby transport incubator for the rescue mission. Travis climbed into the Mercedes van where he busied himself with a tablet computer to produce three Allied Hospital Equipment Ltd company identity badges based on the ones he had taken from the two lads, using a special graphics program on the tablet, with substituted photos and names for himself, Charlie and Sandor. They had all been wearing the close-fitting rubber masks when the photos had been taken. An instant camera was used to produce the badges themselves.

Meanwhile, Charlie and Graham helped Sandor to transfer the baby transport incubator to the Allied Hospital Equipment van. The incubator was now fully operational on its internal power supply. When everything was ready, Sandor and Charlie put on the tabards taken from the two lads and fixed the newly-made identity badges to them. Travis donned a similar-looking tabard, onto which he had stencilled the company's name, and also attached an identity badge. The three of them climbed into the Allied Hospital Equipment van, with Travis driving. Anne, Kevin and Graham watched them set off. For Anne in particular, this was a moment of maximum anxiety. Either she would shortly be seeing her baby, or everything would be lost. It would be all or nothing.

The local one-way system required Travis to make a circuit via Judd Street and Euston Road in order to approach the National Children's Infirmary from Upper Woburn Place and Tavistock Square. He passed the main entrance on Tavistock Square and turned into the approach to the service entrance at the back of the building from Tavistock Place. Travis got out of the van and went into the reception office for the service entry. He presented the paperwork and manifest that the two lads had had with them.

"We've come to deliver these items," he said and pushed the papers across the counter. "We're also to collect an item for repair."

The man behind the counter looked at the paperwork and then at his computer screen and nodded.

"The Supplies Department is along the corridor and through the second set of double doors on the left," he said.

"OK. We're just unloading now."

The man nodded and looked at the time on his computer screen. He could have done without these people arriving just now, as he was about to knock off for his lunch.

Travis went back outside, where Charlie and Sandor had just unloaded the baby transport incubator from the van. The incubator was on its own trolley and was covered with a cloth. Charlie closed and locked the van, and they wheeled the incubator into the service entrance. At the reception office, they presented their identity badges, and the man behind the counter opened the security doors for them. They wheeled the incubator through and along the corridor.

Some way down the corridor they paused next to an alcove which gave access to male and female toilets. Travis reached under the cloth covering the incubator and retrieved a white lab coat from a rack at the bottom of the trolley. Charlie casually looked up and down the corridor and gave a nod. Travis stepped into the alcove and quickly put the lab coat on over the tabard. From his pocket, he produced an NHS identity badge which he had created for himself from a template he had copied and modified for this mission. He stepped back into the corridor. Within thirty seconds, Charlie and Sandor had followed suit. They were now three hospital staff with a piece of equipment for one of the wards.

From the ground floor, they took the lift up to the second floor. On the second floor, there were a number of people in the lift area, but no one took any notice of them as they walked out of the lift, with Charlie wheeling the incubator on its trolley. Travis and Charlie walked together, with Travis holding doors open for Charlie. Sandor walked a little distance behind them to create the impression that he wasn't connected with them. They went through a set of double doors and along a corridor. After the start of the legal proceedings, Emma had been moved to a small, single-bed room on her own in preparation for her life support being switched off as soon as the courts gave the go-ahead. Sandor's most recent visit to Emma had been in this room, and the visit had also been useful for recording information about the room's layout, location and other details.

They went through another set of double doors. As they approached the door to Emma's room, Travis indicated to Charlie that they should slow and stop. A nurse was approaching them along the corridor. Travis reached under the cloth into the rack at the bottom of the trolley, pretending to search for something until the nurse had passed and gone through the double doors.

As soon as she had done so, he went to the door to Emma's room and keyed the entry code into the security lock's keypad. On his previous visit, when the nurse had keyed the code in, Sandor had covertly recorded her doing so on his phone. Travis had then slowed the images down so that he could record the number. After another quick look up and down the corridor, he opened the door just enough to slide into the room. He reached up and popped a small, black plastic bag over the security camera mounted just above the door. He then held the door open for Charlie to wheel the incubator through. A few moments later, Sandor entered the room and closed the door. Travis removed the cover from the incubator and put it on a chair. He moved the incubator next to Emma's bed as directed by Sandor.

At that moment, the door suddenly opened again, and a nurse came in. It was the same nurse who had passed them in the corridor. She had evidently become suspicious and returned to carry out a check.

"Who are you, and what are you doing here?" she demanded.

Travis had remained standing in the middle of the room. He stepped towards the nurse and produced the revolver which had previously been used by Graham. He pointed the revolver at the nurse's face.

"Stay very still. Put your hands up where I can see them and keep quiet, otherwise I'll blow your head off.

This is fully loaded, and I have no problem about using it. We're not going to be stopped now, and no one will find your body until after we've gone."

As Graham had done previously, he pulled the hammer back, making an audible click. Shocked by the revolver, which was clearly real, the nurse did as she was told. Charlie had remained behind the door. He stepped forward with one of the anaesthetic masks and clamped it over the nurse's face. Travis helped Charlie to catch her as she collapsed. The reel of duct tape was retrieved from the rack under the incubator, and Charlie quickly taped the nurse up. Travis held her hands behind her back while Charlie taped her wrists. They moved her into an equipment closet and closed the closet door. Charlie took up his position behind the door again.

"Don't let it faze you," Travis said to Sandor. "We'll deal with any problems like this. It's what we're good at."

Sandor nodded. If there were any two men in the entire world whom he could rely on at that moment, he knew it was these two. He focused his mind on the job in hand. The incident had emphasised that time was of the essence now. He put a mask on, washed his hands with an alcohol wash and put on a fresh pair of latex gloves. The first task was to check Emma's condition. He quickly looked at the monitor readings. Emma's condition had deteriorated slightly since his most recent visit, but she was still well enough to receive his treatment. He asked Travis to move the incubator right alongside the bed and open the top of the incubator. Sandor checked the monitor leads and intravenous feed tube attached to Emma. There was enough slack to move her, so he gently lifted her up and moved her into the incubator. He detached the intravenous tube from the bedside feed and attached it to the incubator's own feed. He then attached Emma to the incubator's own monitors. Emma was now completely supported by the incubator's own systems.

Finally, he located the power cables for the bedside monitors and asked Travis to switch the power off at the wall sockets. It was then safe to detach the bedside monitors from Emma without triggering the alarms. After a quick check to confirm that everything was properly set up, including that the incubator's small internal light was on – Emma was sleeping, but might become distressed if she woke up in the dark – he asked Travis to close the top of the incubator again. Travis then retrieved the cover and placed it back over the incubator. Sandor nodded to Travis to indicate that everything was ready.

Travis opened the door to the corridor slightly and listened for footsteps or any other sounds from the corridor. Hearing nothing, he took a discreet look up and down the corridor. There was no one in sight at that moment, so he opened the door wide for Charlie to push the incubator out into the corridor. Sandor and Travis quickly followed, Travis closing the door behind him. A couple of minutes later, they were back in the lift area, Travis and Charlie with the incubator and Sandor a little distance behind. As before, no one took any particular interest in them as they waited for a lift to arrive.

When they got into a lift, two nurses got in with them, but they were engaged in conversation and took no particular notice of them. The nurses both got out at the first floor. On the ground floor, they paused along the corridor next to the alcove as before. In less than a minute, they were transformed from hospital staff to Allied Hospital Equipment Ltd staff.

The controlled entry and exit door at the reception office for the service entry was a potential problem if any alarm had been raised, which might necessitate the use of force. But evidently no alarm had yet been raised, as no attempt was made to stop them. The door was opened for them, and they showed their passes to be checked out. There was now a different man in the reception office. The man who had let them in was now away for his lunch.

Outside, they carefully loaded the incubator, still with its cover on, into the van. Sandor and Charlie stayed in the back of the van with the incubator while Travis drove. As he turned out of the approach to the service entry onto Tavistock Place, Travis pressed a button on the small radio device, which had been placed on the dashboard, sending out a coded signal. Four hundred yards away, in the underground garage off Wakefield Street, the device in Graham's hand emitted a beep and displayed the coded signal.

"Right, they've done it," Graham said. "They'll be here in a couple of minutes."

He got into the Ford van and backed it out into the parking area, and then got into the Toyota and parked it in the garage. He locked the car, and then opened the sliding side door on the Ford van. Moments later there was the sound of a vehicle approaching down the ramp. It was the Allied Hospital Equipment van. Graham indicated to Travis that everything was ready. Travis paused the van to allow Graham to open the van's sliding side door. Travis then parked the van right alongside the Ford van, with the two sliding side doors open and facing each other. Charlie and Sandor transferred the incubator into the Ford van, where Charlie secured it. As soon as this was done, Travis moved the Allied Hospital Equipment van out of the way. Anne and Kevin climbed into the Ford van with Sandor and Charlie. Travis had explained to them that there would be no time for them to look at Emma before they set off. At that point, speed was vital. But Sandor said:

"We've got her. She's going to make it!"

Anne nodded without speaking. She looked at Travis. This man ...

Travis climbed into the Ford van, holding the gate control. With its doors closed and everything in place, the Ford van, driven by Charlie, immediately set off. At the gates, Travis climbed out and opened the gates, and the Ford van was then on its way. Thirty seconds later, the Mercedes van, driven by Graham, came up the ramp and passed through the gates, following the Ford van. Travis walked back down to the garage.

15

From Tavistock Place, Charlie drove via Gray's Inn Road, High Holborn and Kingsway to Waterloo Bridge, crossing the river there. From Kennington Park Road it was a straight run through to Merton High Street, then south onto the A24. As he drove, Charlie was listening to a pocket radio through an earpiece. It was one of a number of special radio devices that they used on many missions. This one was able to tune into UK police radio frequencies, enabling the listener to eavesdrop on police radio traffic. It would increase the chances of getting advanced warning of any pursuit.

Behind him, in the back of the van, Sandor temporarily removed the cover from the incubator so that Anne and Kevin could see their baby again. Emma was still asleep.

"I've given her a mild sedative via the feed to keep her sedated for the duration of the journey," Sandor explained.

For Anne in particular, this was an unforgettable moment, and she wept with emotion. Even though they were not safe yet, she now sensed strongly that they were going to succeed.

The journey south was uneventful, with Charlie following the A24 down to Worthing, and then the A27 to Shoreham. He turned off the A27 onto the approach road to Shoreham airport and, after a short distance, pulled into the entrance to a disused section of road and parked. A few minutes later, Graham drove past in the Mercedes van. Charlie waited for a few more minutes before following Graham down the approach road.

The main entrance to the airport was midway along the airport perimeter road on the south side of the airport. On each side of the main entrance was a row of aircraft hangars and industrial sheds which backed onto the perimeter road and faced onto the ramp inside the airport proper. The gaps between the hangars and sheds were closed off by gates which separated the airport's airside from the perimeter road. A short section of roadway led to each set of gates from the perimeter road, through the gaps between the hangars. The gates were locked, but they were all fairly low, about a metre or so high, and easily climbable.

One set of gates was not flush with the front of the hangars but set back by a couple of metres. Charlie turned off the perimeter road onto the short section of roadway which led to this set of gates. He pulled into the side alongside the hanger on the left-hand side of the roadway. Just over a minute later, there was a beep from the radio device which had been placed on top of the dashboard. It was a coded signal from Graham to advise that he had now cleared airport security and customs and was about to drive through to the airport's airside.

Charlie pulled out and drove towards the gates, swinging round in a wide turn to the left as he did so. He positioned the van across the roadway alongside the gates, then slowly reversed up to the side of the hangar on the right-hand side of the roadway. Moments later, Graham pulled the Mercedes van in alongside the gates on the other side, parallel with the Ford van. The space between the two vans, which included the gates, was now screened from view from all sides.

Charlie got out and opened the Ford van's sliding side door facing the gates. He climbed in, released the incubator and moved it towards the open door. Everyone then climbed out of the van. Anne and Kevin climbed over the gates. Meanwhile, Graham slid across to the passenger side of the Mercedes van, got out and opened the van's left side sliding door. Charlie and Sandor lifted the incubator out of the Ford van, lifted it over the gates and passed it to Graham and Kevin, who then lifted it into the Mercedes van. Sandor climbed over the gates and, with Anne and Kevin, climbed into the Mercedes van. Graham closed the sliding door and climbed back into the cab via the passenger door. Once in the driving seat, he immediately pulled away onto the airport ramp. Charlie had meanwhile closed the Ford van's side door and climbed back into the cab. He also immediately moved off, turning back down the short section of roadway and back onto the perimeter road. The whole operation took less then two minutes.

After pulling away from the gates, Graham drove the short distance to where Keith Brown was waiting with the Bell helicopter, parked on a concrete hardstand projecting out from the north side of the ramp. Keith had already carried out all the pre-flight checks and procedures and had obtained provisional permission for take-off from the tower, advising that he was just waiting for a delivery item to clear security and customs. Keith had also received the coded signal sent out by Travis as he was leaving the National Children's Infirmary, giving him the heads-up to prepare the helicopter for flight. A further signal from Graham indicated that the arrival of the two vans at Shoreham was imminent.

Keith had aligned the helicopter roughly north-east-south-west, so that the port side passenger door was facing away from the airport buildings. He had also fastened sunshades to the starboard cabin windows. Graham drove the Mercedes van round the front of the helicopter and pulled up alongside the aircraft's port side. The space in between was thus largely hidden from view. Both the port side doors were open, with Keith standing beside the open cockpit door.

Graham got out and walked round to the left side of the van. After a quick look round, he opened the sliding side door. One by one, Anne, Kevin and Sandor got out.

"Keep low, and stay low down when you're in the helicopter," Graham told them.

Within seconds, all three of them were in the helicopter. Keith helped Graham lift the incubator out of the van and into the helicopter. Graham also loaded the box containing a heart monitor, which was the 'official' cargo being delivered to the helicopter. Keith secured the incubator in place in the helicopter's cabin. With the cabin door closed, Keith prepared to climb into the cockpit. Graham closed the van door.

"Good luck!" he said.

Keith nodded and smiled.

Graham climbed back into the driving seat. He turned the van and drove round the front of the helicopter, onto the ramp and back to the airport main entrance. Again, the whole operation had taken less than two minutes.

Sitting in the cockpit, Keith started the helicopter's engines. Whilst listening to them spooling up, he called the tower to request permission for take-off. When he was satisfied with the engines, he engaged the rotors, which began to turn. After a minute, the controller responded to confirm permission and to advise course and altitude. Keith opened the throttles for take-off power and, after listening to the engines for another minute, and taking a quick look round to ensure everything was clear, he moved the pitch control until the rotors took effect. The helicopter lifted smoothly off the hardstand, moving forwards as it did so. Climbing, Keith flew east, until he was clear of the airport buildings, and then turned south.

16

For the authorities, the first sign of trouble emerged at about 12.50, with a phone call to Surrey Police from a householder in Ottershaw who said that he had found two men bound and gagged in his garden shed. Police attended the house about half an hour later. The householder was mystified about how the two men – both of them just young lads – could have got into the shed, both doors of which were padlocked. The two lads, once they regained consciousness, had been unable to free themselves from the tape that Graham had bound them with. One of them had managed to shuffle across the shed floor to one of the doors, which he then started kicking to make a noise. Eventually, the noise had attracted the attention of the householder, who went to investigate. He returned to the house to retrieve the keys to the shed and was astonished to find two men bound and gagged on the shed floor.

After releasing them from the tape, the householder took them back to the house, where he called the police. After the lads had told their story, the police searched the area along the lane but found nothing. The police quickly established that there had been no police motorcycle patrol in the area at the time. The police asked the lads what they had been carrying in the van. The lads answered that it had been items of medical equipment for a hospital in London. But these items had been found in the shed, identified by the lads, and still in their boxes.

At first, the police assumed that the motive behind the incident was simply theft of the van. No particular significance was attached to the van's destination at that point. But the two lads also reported that their company identity badges and the company tabards they wore were missing, as were their mobile phones.

By this time, events were taking place elsewhere. At 1.45, a nurse at the National Children's Infirmary had gone into Emma's room to carry out a routine check, only to find that Emma was not there. The bed was empty, and all the bedside monitors had been switched off. Puzzled, the nurse had then gone to the ward sister to ask what had happened. The ward sister had heard of no plan to move Emma and had contacted the Infirmary's administration. Administration knew that there was no plan to move Emma and that something was wrong. They contacted the consultant in charge of Emma's case, and he knew nothing about it. The senior administrator, Brett Morrison, went with the ward sister to Emma's room to look for himself. They were joined by the consultant, Bahadur Choudhry.

"It looks as if the baby has been abducted," Choudhry said after inspecting the bed and bedside equipment. "Whoever did this knew what they were doing. The power to the monitors has been switched off to prevent the alarms from going off."

"But how was this possible?" Morrison asked. "We have building security and room security. How have they got past that?"

The ward sister, looking around the room, noticed the black plastic bag over the security camera over the door.

"Look," she said, pointing to it.

The others stared at it.

"Don't touch it," said Choudhry. "There may be fingerprints on it. Had the parents scheduled a visit for today?"

"A visit's been scheduled for this evening but not during the day," the ward sister confirmed.

"But they've obviously managed to get in somehow and abduct the baby," said Morrison. "How has that been possible?"

It was another worry for the ward sister. She was already dealing with the problem of a nurse who had failed to report in after her lunch break and who could not be traced. She hadn't taken the matter any higher yet, but that would soon be unavoidable. At that moment, there was a noise from an equipment closet at the side of the room. The noise came again. It sounded like a muffled human voice. Choudhry walked over and opened the closet door and was startled to find a nurse, bound and gagged with duct tape. The ward sister's problem of the missing nurse had been solved.

They released the nurse and sat her on a chair to recover. Choudhry, examining her, found that she had not been seriously harmed. When she was sufficiently recovered, the nurse told her story. When asked, she said that she hadn't recognised any of the men, although she only got a clear view of one of them – the one who had threatened her with a revolver. She hadn't seen the man behind the door who had clamped a mask over her face. That was the last thing that she remembered.

Morrison immediately contacted administration and told them to call the police. He briefly explained what had happened and told them to treat it as an emergency call. He asked the ward sister to go down to reception at the main entrance and escort the police up to Emma's room as soon as they arrived.

As they were waiting, Morrison observed:

"It's essential that this baby is found and brought back here and that the parents are also apprehended, not least to underline the fact that parents, especially stupid chavs like these two, don't get to defy the medical judgement of a respected institution like this, and still less to defy the will of the courts. I want to see them made an example of, as a warning to other stupid parents who still think that the children they spawn somehow belong to them and that they have 'rights' in relation to them."

The police quickly focused on cctv footage from the Infirmary's security cameras, to see if they could find images of the abductors. The nurse who had been anaesthetised and taped up said that the three men had been wheeling an object on a trolley, apparently a piece of equipment of some kind, with a cover draped over it. It didn't take long to find images that appeared to show the three men and the trolley. The nurse said that they appeared to be the same three men she had seen. As well as images from a camera on the second floor, there were also images from the security camera covering the service entrance at the back of the building, indicating that this was where they had managed to enter the building.

Interviewing the reception office staff at the service entrance, the police established that the three men were apparently making a delivery to the Infirmary from a company called Allied Hospital Equipment Ltd of Woking. The National Children's Infirmary received much of its medical equipment from this company, and visits to the Infirmary by the company's vans were regular and frequent, delivering equipment and collecting equipment for repair. This visit had been scheduled in advance and was expected. The man on duty in the reception office when the van had arrived, and who had let the three men in, said that he hadn't recognised any of the three, although he was familiar with most of Allied Hospital Equipment's regular delivery drivers, but he hadn't thought there was anything particularly significant about that at the time.

The cctv footage from the service entrance provided moderately good images of the three men, and also of the van, showing its registration plate. A plan to visit Allied Hospital Equipment Ltd in Woking was forestalled when a courtesy call to Surrey Police revealed that they were already investigating the hijacking at gunpoint of the same van that morning. A picture was beginning to emerge of how the abduction had been planned and carried out.

Thames Valley Police were also contacted, and requested to visit the parents' address in Didcot. It was assumed that the parents must be involved in some way, even if there was no direct evidence of that yet. This appeared to be confirmed by a report from Thames Valley Police later that day. Having broken into the Nortons' house on getting no response when they knocked at the door, they found the house empty and evidently closed down for a long absence. The police ransacked the house but could find no information about where the Nortons may have gone. They were already widening their search to try to identify and locate other members of the Nortons' family so they could be picked up for questioning. Images of the Nortons, and of the three men from the Infirmary's cctv system, were issued to all ports and airports.

Attention now focused on the search for the Allied Hospital Equipment Ltd van in which the baby had been abducted. Even though it was possible that the abductors may have transferred to another vehicle, this was all the police had to go on at that point. Once Surrey Police had confirmed the registration of the van with Allied Hospital Equipment Ltd, a trawl of data from cctv traffic cameras linked to number plate recognition technology began.

At first, they had no success. The van's vehicle tracking device wasn't responding for some reason. No sightings were reported from traffic cameras either. Travis had switched the LCD plates to show the Allied Hospital Equipment van's actual registration only when waiting in a traffic queue at the lights on Tavistock Square, making sure that there were other vehicles close behind and in front so that the change wouldn't be seen. He had switched back to a false registration at the first set of lights on Tavistock Place after leaving the Infirmary, again in a traffic queue with other vehicles close behind and in front.

Eventually, they got a sighting report. A traffic camera on the A12 just east of Romford was triggered by the van's registration number. It wasn't clear how the van had reached that point without triggering cameras before then, but at least they now had a sighting. Identification was confirmed by a camera at the next set of traffic lights. The van was now approaching Junction 28 on the M25. An armed response team was immediately dispatched in a patrol car from Romford police station in pursuit. A police helicopter was also ordered to be scrambled to try to track the van from the air. Patrol cars already on that section of the M25 were alerted, and Essex Police were also contacted to advise them of the situation.

Information from traffic cameras indicated that the van didn't turn onto the M25 at Junction 28 but continued through the junction: not onto the main A12 Colchester road but onto the smaller A1023 instead. It was making its way into Essex.

17

Travis walked back down the ramp to the garage. Before closing and locking the garage door, he removed a number of items from the Allied Hospital Equipment van and put them in the garage and retrieved a plastic canister full of petrol from the garage and stowed it in the van. With the garage secured, he turned the van round and drove it onto the ramp. He stopped to get out and retrieve the plastic bag covering the security camera. A minute later he was through the gates and turning onto Tavistock Place.

From Tavistock Place, Travis made his way via Sidmouth Street and Gray's Inn Road onto the inner ring road east at King's Cross station, and then via Whitechapel Road onto the A118 eastbound. As he drove, he was listening in to the police radio to catch any information about a pursuit. In Romford, he pulled off the main road into a supermarket car park where he stopped to wait. He sat listening to the police radio, listening for indications about the state of any pursuit. At length, the two things he was waiting for happened within a few minutes of each other. He picked up a general call on the police network to all patrols to look out for the Allied Hospital Equipment Ltd van, giving its correct registration. The call was accompanied by a warning that the occupants of the van were armed and dangerous and any patrol spotting the van should seek advice before proceeding. This call was repeated several times. A short while later, the special radio device, which he had placed on the dashboard, emitted a bleep. It was a coded message from Graham. The code meant that the helicopter had taken off, with Emma, her parents and Sandor aboard.

He fixed a satnav to the dashboard and switched it on, before starting the engine. Back on the main road, in the traffic queue at the first set of traffic lights, he switched the LCD displays to show the van's actual registration number. He was now a sitting duck. He went through several more sets of traffic lights, including at a major junction. At most of these, traffic cameras were visible. He didn't have to wait long before there was a response. A call was put out on the police network to all patrols in the Havering sector that the Allied Hospital Equipment Ltd van had been tracked on the A12 just east of Romford heading towards the M25. As before, the call included the warning that the occupants of the van were armed and dangerous and that any patrol spotting the van should seek further instructions before proceeding.

At this point, Travis was on the A12 approaching Junction 28 on the M25. He needed to get off the A12, which was a dual carriageway with very limited exit opportunities. He joined the traffic queue for the slip road onto the junction. Whilst waiting in the queue, he pressed the button to switch the registration number being displayed on the LCD plates so that he wouldn't be tracked by the cameras going through the junction. Having now got the police on his tail, he didn't want to make it too easy for them. There was heavy traffic on both the A12 and on the slip road for the M25, and the traffic edged forwards agonisingly slowly. As he came up to the traffic lights where the slip road joined the junction roundabout, his attention was caught by flashing blue lights in his mirror. It was the first sighting of the pursuit, although the blue lights were still in the far distance, and the slip road was clogged with traffic. When he moved through the traffic lights onto the roundabout, the blue lights hadn't got much closer.

A few minutes later, he was approaching the exit onto the A1023, still in heavy traffic on the roundabout. As he did so, his attention was caught by more flashing blue lights, which he could see through the underpass beneath the motorway. As far as he could see, this was a vehicle which was on the slip road exiting the northbound carriageway of the M25 as it approached the roundabout on the other side of the motorway. He could hear the vehicle's siren as it tried to get through the heavy traffic. A minute later, he again saw flashing blue lights in his mirror. This time they were on the exit slip road from the southbound carriageway of the M25 coming down to the roundabout behind him. It was still in the distance, having just exited the motorway, and there was heavy traffic on the slip road. It looked as if the police were converging on Junction 28 in the hope of catching him there.

Seconds later, Travis exited the junction onto the A1023. The A1023 here was just a local road which led into the small town of Brentwood. There was a lot less traffic on this road, so he was now able to make better progress. He followed the road into the centre of Brentwood. At the main junction in the centre of the town, he turned left onto Ongar Road, which led north out of Brentwood. While waiting in the traffic at this junction, he switched the LCD plates to display the van's correct registration before going through the junction. In a queue at traffic lights at a junction on the northern edge of the town, he again briefly switched the LCD plates to display the van's correct registration as he went through the junction. There was at least one camera covering the junction. After crossing the A1023, Ongar Road continued north-west past Pilgrims' Hatch. Travis was still listening to the police radio but heard no immediate response to the van passing the cameras in Brentwood with its correct registration displayed.

Beyond Pilgrims' Hatch was the Essex countryside, with the road being heavily tree-lined for most of the way. Once out into open country, he felt a little more confident. It looked as if he was controlling the situation satisfactorily. A long, straight stretch of road was followed by a bend in which the road curved round to the right. It was here that Travis ran straight into the ambush. A police car suddenly pulled out of a side road just ahead of him. It came to a stop positioned across the road, blocking it. Its blue lights were flashing. A moment later, Travis saw more blue lights in his mirror as another police car pulled out from somewhere behind him. He hadn't noticed it on passing, so it must have been well hidden. Nor had he heard anything on the police radio, so possibly they were using mobile phones to communicate.

Travis was travelling at about 50mph, and had only a few seconds in which to react. He was about to hit the brakes when he realised that the police car had stopped a little too far across the road, leaving a gap between the back end of the car and the hedge. He kept his foot on the accelerator and aimed for the gap. As he did so, he saw the driver of the police car aiming a gun at him through the open driver's side window. A split second later, he heard a bullet striking the van. Almost simultaneously, he saw that the gap he was aiming for was not quite wide enough. In other circumstances, he would have steered to hit the hedge, but these were no ordinary circumstances.

The police driver fired again, this time clearly aiming to hit him. He didn't allow enough deflection, and Travis heard the bullet striking the van somewhere behind him. Travis steered so that the offside front wing of the van struck the offside rear wing of the police car a glancing blow. The impact toppled the police car onto its side; moments later, it rolled over onto its roof. The van's nearside brushed heavily against the hedge before the van cleared the gap. Still in control, Travis steered back onto the road and accelerated away. The driver of the police car that had pulled out behind Travis stopped to render assistance to his colleagues in the overturned police car. As it happened, they had not been seriously injured and managed to scramble out of the car windows with some assistance. They remained with their crashed vehicle until further assistance arrived, and to close the road at that point, which had now become a crime scene. The other police car then set off in pursuit of the van.

By this time, Travis was some distance away. Having accelerated away from the crash site, he turned right onto a minor road about a quarter of a mile farther on. A curve in the road meant that this was not visible from the crash site. For the moment, it looked as if he had evaded the pursuit. However, that impression was to be very short-lived. A long, straight stretch on the minor road allowed Travis to accelerate. Even as he did so, he became aware of another sound above the noise of the van's engine. Looking up, he saw that there was a police helicopter low overhead. It was keeping pace with him, so it was clearly tracking him. Tall trees all along the road on both sides prevented the helicopter from flying very low or landing, but it was quite obviously keeping pace with the van.

Abruptly, the police car was back behind him again, blue lights blazing and siren going, obviously having been directed to his location by the helicopter crew. Possibly the car had taken a short-cut to reach him so quickly. The police car, being faster, soon caught up with the van. The police then repeatedly tried to overtake, but because the minor road was only narrow, Travis was able to prevent that by swerving from side to side. As they tore along the narrow lane, the van's rear wing collided with the car's front wing several times as Travis swung the van to prevent the car from getting past. As he approached a bend in the road, Travis suddenly slammed the brakes on hard, bringing the van to a halt. Caught by surprise, the police rammed into the back of the van. Travis was jolted back in his seat by the force of the impact. The impact triggered both of the safety airbags in the police car. Travis then accelerated away while the police fought to clear the airbags out of the way. It was nearly a minute before they were able to resume the pursuit.

But the pursuit was relentless. Even though it was now damaged, the police car was still faster and, guided by the helicopter, it managed to catch up with the van again. Travis had turned left onto an even narrower lane. The police car followed, guided by the helicopter. This lane was long and fairly straight, and the police changed their tactics. Instead of trying to overtake, they now opened fire with a gun. Travis heard a bullet striking the van somewhere behind him. He kept swerving to spoil the gunman's aim. Another bullet hit the van.

Suddenly, Travis was approaching a junction, where the end of the lane formed a T-junction with a main road. There was no warning signage, and he was upon the junction almost before he realised it. The lane was flanked on both sides by a continuous, tall thick hedge, right alongside the road on each side, making the lane seem even narrower than it was. The hedges ran right up to the junction, meaning that there was almost no visibility along the main road until one had actually reached it. Travis braked, but not in time to stop at the line at the junction.

The events of the next few seconds seemed to be in the hands of another power. There was no traffic approaching along the main road from the left, but a large articulated petrol tanker wagon was approaching from the right. The wagon was only yards away from the junction. Unable to stop, the van was already out onto the main road by the time Travis had taken in the situation. He steered sharply to the right to try to clear the near-side carriageway. He almost made it, but the tanker wagon clipped the rear wing of the van as it passed. The van started to topple. It ran on its near-side wheels only for a dozen yards or so before it finally toppled. It slid along the road for another few yards before coming to rest on its left side, leaving Travis hanging by his seatbelt.

The police car was only yards behind the van. The driver was so furiously intent on the pursuit that he made no attempt to stop at the junction and followed the van out onto the main road. The warning screamed by the helicopter pilot was to no avail. The side of the police car took the full impact of the tanker wagon moving at 50mph. The two occupants of the police car died instantly as the tanker ploughed over the car, leaving it a flattened, mangled piece of wreckage. Its petrol tank exploded a few seconds later. The tanker driver had started to swing to the left to try and avoid the van. As the tanker ploughed over the police car, the tanker driver lost control, and the tanker jack-knifed. The sheer momentum of the nearly full, thirty-foot-long petrol tank trailer sheared the coupling with the tractor unit. The tractor unit ended up on its right side, facing the way it had come. The detached petrol tank trailer careered on for another fifty yards before toppling and rolling right over, coming to rest lying across the road, with petrol gushing from the ruptured tank.

The helicopter hovered over the scene of the crash as the crew tried to assess the situation, with the co-pilot hoarsely shouting a description of the scene over the helicopter's radio. Seconds later, there was an enormous explosion as the hundreds of gallons of petrol in the ruptured trailer tank ignited. The helicopter was blown out of the air by the force of the explosion. It landed upside down in a field alongside the road. When leaking aviation fuel reached its still-hot engines, it exploded. But the crew were already dead.

A huge mushroom cloud of smoke rose into the air from the exploding petrol tanker. The blast of the explosion had blown away the hedges and trees on either side of the road at that point. Further away, the hedges alongside the road were on fire for some distance on either side, with thick, black smoke billowing up and drifting along the road. Debris from the explosion, including stones and rubble from the crater in the road, began to hit the ground all around.

Miraculously, the tanker driver survived the explosion, protected mainly by the underside of the tractor unit, which was facing the explosion, and the back of the cab. However, the heat from the huge petrol fire was starting to make conditions inside the cab untenable, and dense, black smoke from the fires was getting into the cab through the fractured windows. The hedges on either side of the road were heavily on fire, but the driver could just make out the junction about thirty yards away. He needed to reach it to stay alive. Having freed himself from his seatbelt, he kicked out the front windscreen of the cab and scrambled through. He ran towards the junction. The heat was intense. Within seconds, the back of his jacket and his hair were beginning to singe. When he reached the junction, he ran down the lane for a distance before rolling on the ground to put his singed jacket out. Finally, he sat down on the grass verge under the hedge to try to recover from the shock.

Once he had freed himself from the seatbelt, Travis stood upright on the passenger side door of the van, which now formed the floor with the van on its side. This was the end of the mission, although even he could never have imagined that it would end like this. He retrieved the plastic bag which had been used to cover the surveillance camera in the Wakefield Street garage and put a number of items into it, including the satnav and the special radio device. He also retrieved the plastic canister full of petrol. He kicked out the van's windscreen and stepped out onto the road. He retrieved the LCD plates from the front and back of the van and put them into the plastic bag. The rear plate was broken and mangled by the impact with the police car. At the back of the van, the heat from the burning petrol tanker was intense. At the front of the van, he picked up the plastic canister, sloshed the petrol into and over the van and laid a short ignition trail before throwing the empty canister into the van. The ignition trail proved to be unnecessary. The petrol, ignited by a drifting spark, went up with a whoosh, almost in his face. He grabbed the plastic bag and ran along the road away from the fire. The road was filled with dense smoke from the burning tanker and burning hedges and trees alongside the road. The smoke meant that he was invisible to anyone who might otherwise have observed him. There must have been traffic building up further down the road, which was now blocked by the crash site, but it was invisible in the smoke. Travis could no longer hear the helicopter and wondered what had become of it, not realising that it had also crashed.

A short distance along the road, he came upon a small gap in the hedge, big enough for him to climb through. Beyond the hedge was a grass field, the extent of which was obscured by drifting smoke. However, Travis walked along the edge of the field, keeping close to the hedge to make himself as inconspicuous as possible. He came to a gate in the hedge, which led into the next field. Again, he walked round the edge of the field, keeping close to the hedge. In this way, he traversed several fields, cautiously crossing a lane in the process. Looking back, he could see a huge column of smoke still rising into the sky from the burning tanker and surrounding fires.

After crossing another field, he checked his position on the satnav. This showed that he was now quite close to a road, on the other side of which was a wood. When he reached the hedge that bordered the road, he walked along it until he was directly opposite the wood. After finding a place where he could climb through the hedge, he waited until the road was clear before walking across the road and into the wood. He walked some way into the wood before sitting down on a fallen tree trunk. He retrieved the special radio device from the plastic bag and pressed one of the buttons to send out a coded message. A couple of minutes later, he received an acknowledgement from Charlie. He left the radio device on whilst he sat and waited so that Charlie could locate him.

Sitting resting in the seclusion of the wood, Travis began to experience the reaction to the unwinding of the extreme tension of the events of the last few hours. The day itself had been the culmination of weeks of planning and preparation. The extreme stress of the events of that day, culminating in a desperate pursuit in which he had almost lost his life, was counterbalanced by the knowledge that, barring an unlikely mischance, he had pulled off an extraordinarily successful mission. That was what made everything worthwhile. This was what he lived for. He had defied the power of the state and won.

But now he began to experience the psychological reaction as he sat in the seclusion of this temporary refuge. There could hardly be a greater contrast between this quiet wood and the inferno he had walked away from, a mile or so away. There was almost complete silence in the stillness under the canopy of trees. Where the sunlight touched the tops of the trees, the leaves of the canopy were brilliant with the green of life, dappling the streams of light that reached down to the woodland floor. Against the green of the trees was set the blue, pink, yellow and purple of a profusion of woodland flowers covering the ground. The silence was emphasised by the occasional drumming of a woodpecker echoing through the green stillness. His pulse and breathing slowed as the slant of the sun's light shifted infinitesimally with each passing minute. His attention was caught by movement. A grey squirrel was coming down the trunk of a tree to reach the ground – a fleeting grey flash, and then it was gone amongst the undergrowth. It was a place of infinite peace.

At length, he heard a different kind of movement: the sound of someone walking through the undergrowth of the wood. He got up and took cover behind a bush until he could see who it was. It was Charlie. Travis stood up and walked towards him.

"I've parked on the road at the edge of the wood," Charlie explained.

They walked back to the road and got into the Ford van.

"I've been listening to the radio whilst I was driving down," Charlie said. "It sounds like you've caused a major incident."

Travis grimaced.

"It wasn't planned that way. I misjudged it. They almost got me. They were tracking me with a helicopter, and I couldn't escape. What happened was pure chance – fate, if you like."

"They were saying on the radio that there are four police dead: two in a patrol car and two in a helicopter."

"The helicopter...?"

"It was apparently brought down by the explosion."

"I didn't realise that. I was wondering what had happened to it."

"No regrets?"

Travis shook his head.

"They were trying to kill me. The two in the police car were armed and shooting into the back of the van as they pursued me. They had no regrets. They died in the service of their cause, which in this case was to ensure that little Emma Norton was denied the chance of life. I can only trust that they would have regarded their lives as having been justifiably expended. So – no regrets."

Charlie merely nodded, and then started the engine.

Six hundred miles to the south, Keith Brown brought the Bell helicopter in to land on the helipad of the *Aegiale* as it rode a gentle Mediterranean swell. For Emma, this was to be a time to live.

Carl Richardson
18th May 2023

This book is printed on paper from sustainable sources managed under the Forest Stewardship Council (FSC) scheme.

It has been printed in the UK to reduce transportation miles and their impact upon the environment.

For every new title that Troubador publishes, we plant a tree to offset CO_2, partnering with the More Trees scheme.

MORE TREES
LET'S PLANT A BILLION TREES

For more about how Troubador offsets its environmental impact, see www.troubador.co.uk/sustainability-and-community